Shadow Warriors

Tome 1 : Burning Love

Sharon Kena

traduit du français par Lisa Angelini

Les Editions Sharon Kena

©2014Les Editions Sharon Kena

www.leseditionssharonkena.com
ISBN : 978-2-36540-616-1

CHAPTER 1

For the first time since they started going out in the evening, Camilla and Angeline decide to try a new place. Tonight, they aren't going to the *Retro* as they usually do, but to another bar Angeline has heard of through her co-workers, called *Byzance*. Apparently, the place is very popular and crowded every night. On arrival there, they realise how packed it is indeed, but soon manage to find a spare table left behind by a group.

The music is quite loud and different from what they usually listen to. It sounds like a mix between metal, gothic rock and hardcore punk that gets people dancing. Angeline shots glances at all the partiers inside the bar. Again, they're all pretty different from the well-groomed, good-mannered people she usually comes across. The women – most of which are shortly dressed – are swaying their hips on the dancefloor and seem to be in their element. The men are sitting down, drinking beer or other alcoholic beverages. A few of them are dancing with their female partner or some girl they just met. And there is...

Him.

Seated at a table with three other men, he drinks the rest of his glass in one go and their eyes meet. She is hypnotized instantaneously. He seems tall and has broad shoulders, a dark face... but he's also incredibly handsome and mysterious. His beauty is bewitching.

"You go order our drinks," Camilla says.

Immersed in her contemplation of the attractive stranger, Angel does not hear a single word.

"Angel!"

"Yes." Her eyes dart to her friend.

"Do you want to order?"

Still lost in her own world, Angel needs a moment to collect her thoughts. It seems like an eternity, but only lasts one second. She was so fascinated by that guy over there!

"Yeah, I'll go."

She gets up and makes her way towards the crowded counter. Two bartenders are standing behind it, overwhelmed by the demands of their thirsting customers and she has to wait a few minutes before one of them notices her. "What are you having?"

"Two Desperados in glasses, please."

The bartender pours the beers in two glasses, adds a slice of lemon on each, takes her money and moves on to the next customer. Angel grabs a mug in each hand and slowly spins around, her eyes focused on the drinks. She doesn't see that there is someone standing behind her, and bumps right into them. The drinks hit the man's stomach, splashing his black tank top.

"Be careful for God's sake!"

His loud and angry voice makes her want to disappear, and she barely dares to look up at him to apologize. But as she meets the giant's gaze, the words refuse to come out.

It's him.

His face is tense and he looks as if he is going to pounce on her at any moment. Incredibly good-looking. An electric shock runs through her entire body.

"I'm sorry," she finally mutters.

"Well, you can be," he growls.

"Enough now Kral, you're scaring the lady," the bartender who just served her intervenes.

Kral shots a, intimidating look at the man. Angel swallows the lump in her throat. She is standing in front of the handsome man she was staring at a few minutes ago, and she has already given him a poor impression. She must find a way to make up for it.

"I'll clean up the mess!" she blurted out unintentionally. She feels like a total dork. And the dark, threatening look he gives her doesn't help. He begins to take his top off and she muffles a cry. Everything happens very quickly. She sees his muscular stomach and assumes he must spend his time in weights rooms, and she just has the time to catch a glimpse of the scar on his torso.

"Stop it, Kral. Or all the chicks in the room are gonna faint," the bartender laughs.

Kral puts his top back in place. Angel is pretty sure he would have taken if off completely if it wasn't for the barman's comment. How belittling is that word anyway, *chicks*? His dark eyes are on her again and she is petrified. There isn't the hint of a smile on his face. She waits for him to speak, but no words come out of his mouth. She dreads the moment he will walk back to his table. She must hold him back... again.

"I can do it in the bathroom."

What an idiot!

"Do... what?" he asks with a surprised look on his face.

"Clean it up."

She seriously needs to stop acting like such an uptight idiot. She may not be as outgoing as Camilla, she can usually string two words together. But this hot giant just makes her lose control. And apparently, it doesn't really make her look her best.

"Did you hear that?" he says to the bartender before turning his face to Angel,"I don't want you to pass out."

What a jerk!

What does he take her for? If she was a tad taller and if her hands were free, she'd slap him in the face. Without smiling or even apologizing, he orders a glass of something. The bartender serves him his drink whilst Angel is still standing there, as if waiting for something. She wants to head back to her table, but her legs feel like cotton wool and won't move.

"Whatcha waitin' for?" Kral barks.

"Hum, nothing."

"Good. Because I don't date the prostitutes in this town."

"..."

She tries to come up with a sharp comeback, but he disappears through the crowd with his drinks before she even has the time to open her mouth. She gets back to her table, vexed and angry that he thinks she might be that sort of person.

"So many people in here!" Camilla exclaims.

Angel nods and puts the drinks on the high stainless steel table.

"Gosh, they're so stingy... The glasses are only half-full!"

Indeed, Angel notices that she has spilled nearly half of their beers on Kral. What a strange name! She quickly tells her friend about what happened. She gave him such a bad impression, she's pretty convinced it's hopeless. Did she ever stand a chance anyway?

"Where the heck is that jerk?" Camilla asks when she is done telling her the story.

Angel automatically looks in the direction of the table where he is still seated with his three friends. Camilla observes him and makes a comment about his intimidating looks. She advises Angel against it, but the latter knows it's pointless. It's too late anyway. She looks away, not wanting him to catch her staring.

The young woman forgets about Kral during the two following hours, focusing on Camilla and their girl talk. The two friends often see each other, but they always find something to talk about. They've known each other for years and are as close as sisters. The word "best friends" isn't strong enough to describe them.

"I'm just going to go to the bathroom and then we can leave," Angel decides.

It's nearly midnight, and the pretty girl with the long black hair feels exhausted. As she expected it, the restroom is packed, and she must wait in line. Her mind wanders off for a moment and she wonders if Kral is still here or has already left. She probably won't see him again... unless she comes back here. The bartender seemed to know him quite well, so he must be a regular customer.

She is now in front of the line and it is her turn to relieve herself. Three bathroom stalls for the whole pub isn't enough! She's never seen so many people in such a tiny place. As she makes her way out, her gaze meet the reflection of a tall man standing against the white marble sinks. Kral.

What is he doing here?

Ths is definitely the ladies' room!

"I accept your offer," he says before taking his tank top off.

She is speechless. What a perfect body! Without a doubt, it was the most muscular and sexiest torso in the whole wide world . He puts his top down on the sink although it would have been wiser to give it to her directly. At least, she now has an answer to her question: he hasn't left yet.

"Hum, sure," she says, getting closer to the attractive stranger.

She is angry at herself. She needs to let him know how she feels, to make him understand that she finds him very attractive and that she isn't the kind of person he thinks. However, her body refuses to comply and she grabs the tank top with both hands. Before she realizes what is happening, she is sitting down on the ledge of the sink with Kral standing between her thighs. She holds her breath as he takes the tank top from her hands, which he then places on his sculptural torso. What does he want? What is he looking for? Those questions should have crossed her mind, but instead, she finds herself caressing that man she doesn't know. His skin is incredibly soft but also firm. She trails her fingers across his scar, which starts on the left side of his chest and ends on his left. She is eager to find out what happened to him, but she is even more eager to discover the rest of his body. Again, no words come out. She looks up at the man she desires. His dark piercing eyes, his black tousled hair, the stubble on his jaw, his eyebrow piercing... He *must* be aware of how attractive he is. He's so tall and imposing she feels like a fragile little thing, even more so when he pulls her against him and seals her lips with a kiss. She doesn't push him away, but abandons herself in the kiss, in his embrace. She feels his hands slide up

8

her naked thighs and underneath her skirt as he deepens the kiss. Entirely under the influence of her desire, she lets him take possession of her body and they fuse for a relatively short, but inexorably delicious moment.

She feels weak as he pulls out, and only realizes that she just had sex with a total stranger when she sees him zipping up his jeans. He grabs her by the waist to put her back on her feet but she is a bit wobbly. She assumes he's going to say something, but he simply puts his top back on and leaves the room after unlocking the door.

What an idiot!

Sleeping with a stranger without taking any precautions... how irresponsible! And he just left her there, to top it all off. Now she knows for sure what kind of person he takes her for... which on that moment, makes her feel like a nobody.

Girls keep swarming into the bathroom. Angel feels their stares and hurries out of the room to join Camilla.

"Finally! I was wondering where you were."

Angel doesn't answer. She sits down and accidentally meets Kral's eyes, who is staring at her. She can't look away. He looks at her, chewing on a toothpick, which makes him look even sexier! Seriously, he could do anything and still look hot. But she doesn't like the satisfied look on his face at all. She imagines herself getting up, walking towards their table, grabbing the glass in front of him and throwing it in his face. But this will remain a fantasy, I'm afraid.

"Angel!"

The young woman turns her head to face Camilla at the sound of her name.

"Don't tell me you actually like this guy."

"I do."

By saying it out loud, she knows it is true. She's always been attracted to macho, contemptuous guys, so why not him? Except this time, something is different. It's not just a simple attraction, but as if her heart was whispering to her *"It's him"* and she couldn't do anything against it.

"I don't like him."

"I just had sex with him."

Camilla's eyes widen. Angel perfectly understands her surprise: she doesn't usually act this way. And still! Kral could make her do anything.

CHAPTER 2

Camilla anxiously waits for David. It is the fourth time they go on a date tonight. She really likes the guy, and she intends to take their relationship to the next level. They were going to go see a thriller at the cinema tonight, but David called her to cancel. He didn't really give her an explanation and told her he had something urgent to do. Of course, she was disappointed and he must have heard it in her voice, because he suggested they should meet later at *Retro*.

"Hey."

Camilla looks up at the handsome dark-haired guy with broad shoulders. She smiles at him as he sits down across from her.

"I hope you haven't been waiting for too long."

"I just got here."

"What do you feel like drinking?"

"A Coke."

He gestures to the waitress and orders their drinks: a Coke and a beer. Camilla observes him as he does so. He doesn't look anything like the burly guy with piercing dark eyes Angel has a crush on. David is a smiling person and doesn't exude anything but sweetness. She met him in this very place, ten days ago. She was with Angel, and he was with three of his friends: Kevin, Bastien and Alan. A group of twenty-five year-old welcoming and funny young lads. The girls had joined him and they had spent a great evening.

Since then, Camilla and David had been seeing each other from time to time. She knows nothing about him, apart from the fact that he is in the military and a night owl who loves to party.

"Do you want to dance?" he asks her after the waitress brought them their drinks.

"Okay."

Being on the dancefloor in David's arms makes her feel a bit odd. She was upset about him cancelling the cinema but it wasn't such a bad thing after all. Plus, he promised he would take her to see a movie very soon to make it up to her. After a few dances, they go back to their table and Camilla wonders if they're going to be alone the rest of the night. Usually, David's friends join them at some point... Well, "they invite themselves", to be more accurate. And they probably will tonight, which is why she wanted to go see a movie.

"I'm really sorry I had to change our plans."

"I know David, you've already apologized."

She loves the warm, velvety tone he uses when speaking to her.

"We'll go tomorrow, I promise," he says, putting his hand over hers.

An electric shock runs down her spine as he caresses the top of her hand and intertwines his fingers with hers. She tries to breathe normally, but it is impossible. Her heart is pounding inside her chest. "Do you think your friends might come?"

It's the only question she could come up with to take her mind off his warm palm.

"No. I asked them to give us some space tonight."

He smiles and so does she. He wants to be alone with her: nothing could make her feel happier. Her eyes drift down to their hands, thinking that if he wants them to be alone, he must feel the same way as she does. He made a step towards her, it's her turn now. Without letting go of his hand, she moves closer to him. He doesn't look surprised, which encourages her to keep on. She puts her other hand on their interlaced fingers and feels compelled to kiss him, but she is scared it might be too soon. She doesn't want to go too fast and scare him off. Camilla is a bit sentimental and she likes perfect love stories, from beginning to end.

Her blue eyes sink into David's. His are brown, warm and beautiful. She doesn't hear the music anymore and feels like they are in their own little world. They look at each other for a short moment, before David leans in to kiss her. She kisses him back unrestrainedly. Both in their own bubble, separated from the outside world and everybody in the club, they kiss. With her eyes closed, Camilla enjoys the touch of the man she desires, one of his hands on her face and the other in her hair.

Everything happens quite naturally after the kiss. David and Camilla exit the club and go back to his place, not too far away. They have only just stepped into the flat when he seals their lips for another feverish kiss. No words are exchanged as she finds herself lying down on the young man's double bed.

As she was getting ready for their date, Camilla had never imagined it would end this way, even though it had crossed her mind. The young man spends some time lingering on her body, turning her on to the maximum, before taking possession of her body with exquisite gentleness.

Angel had been trying to get through to Camilla all evening, without success. She knows that her friend is with David, but she was hoping they wouldn't be too long. Or maybe she could join them in the club and find the man she lusts for. She wants to go to *Byzance* and see him again, but not alone. She would be too terrified. She needs her sister to be there too, but apparently, Camilla is too busy to pick up her phone. She isn't mad at her friend as she's aware of her feelings for David, but it doesn't change anything to the problem. She *has* to see him.

Kral.

She hadn't stopped thinking about him since she had met his gaze for the first time the day before. Of course, they had shared more than just glances, but he had walked away! He had taken her for the kind of girl who... but what had happened represented so much more! What would he think if he saw her hanging out at *Byzance* again? He makes her lose control and self-confidence. She can't let that happen and let him think such things about her! She must see him and make things right.

Standing in front of *Byzance*, Angel's mind is on overdrive. *Is he in there or not?* The question seems insignificant compared to: should I stay or should I leave? Never before had a man made her doubt herself like this. Kral seems so unattainable and yet she desires him more than anything else. It is as if something inside her is pushing her in his arms. But what it is and why it is there, she doesn't know.

She finally enters the bar, and her eyes dart here and there until she sits down at the counter. Seems like the one she's looking for isn't there... but she doesn't dare to look again.

"Hey, I know you," says the bartender from the previous day.

She nods before ordering a vodka. Seems like he's got a good visual memory.

"I'm surprised you came back. I hope Kraler didn't freak you out. He's... himself," he smiles.

Kraler. So that's what he's called. Kral must be the short version.

"No, don't worry. I'm waiting for a friend," she replies, shooting a look at her phone.

The barman serves her the vodka, takes her money and gets on with his business while she tries to call Camilla yet another time. She still naively hopes that her friend will join her. At least, she wouldn't have to wait alone.

Voicemai. She hangs up and distracts herself with her drink for a moment before downing it as the bartender comes back to her.

"Isn't your friend supposed to join you?"

"She's late and won't pick up her phone."

"I'm sure she'll be here any minute."

Angel lets out a sigh. She knows he's wrong, but it's probably best if he believes so as she would hate for him to think she came back here for a man. Kraler.

The barman smiles at her. "I'm Stefan."

"Angel."

He serves a drink to a customer who just arrived at the counter. Angel glances at him mechanically. She knows him for she has seen him somwhere before. He's muscular, blond, and seems quite uncongenial.

"Hey Friz!"

When she sees him shaking the bartender's hand, Angel remembers having seen him with Kral the night before, he is one of his three friends. If that guy called Friz is there, Kral mustn't be too far. She has to refrain from turning around and go over the place with a fine-tooth comb. Wouldn't it be embarrassing if she met his gaze? He would probably imagine she came back for him. Pathetic! That's exactly the case, though. So much for trying to play the mysterious and unattainable girl. Her attention is back to her phone when Stefan offers, "Another vodka?"

"That would be nice. I just got stood up."

"Who would dare?" asks a voice coming from behind her.

Her head turns as the man sits down on her left. "Give me a whisky, Stefan."

Kraler.

Angel cannot find the words. She can't believe he is there beside her when he seemed so far away just a few moments ago.

Mysterious and unattainable.

The words play over and over again in her head but she is unable to put up a front.

Kral's eyes are on her. He is waiting for an answer and she hates herself for losing all her confidence.

"A friend."

He has no reaction. No fair. It took her all she had to string these two words together! She watches as he downs his drink, hoping he will demonstrate some kind of interest towards her but he simply strolls away. She spins around to see him join Friz at a table not too far from where she is. She pulls herself together quickly before he sees him. She definitely doesn't want him to think she's there for him... as obvious as it may seem.

Yet again, she tries to call Camilla but gives up at the sound of her answering machine. Stefan gives her a sympathetic look. Time to face reality: she's going to spend the evening alone and might as well go back home.

"Another vodka?"

"No thanks. I'm going home."

"Sorry your friend didn't show up."

"She probably had better things to do."

She smiles at the bartender and turns on her heels. Her eyes automatically drift to the table where Kraler is sitting with Friz and two other men. Not only two other men, though. He is lounging on his chair, a cigar at the corner of his lips, his eyes focused on a blonde who is giving him a lap dance.

Angel is boiling with rage. She feels like a complete idiot for having this sort of feeling toward such a rude man. Tearing her eyes off him, she exits the bar.

Once in the street, she inhales deeply. She never should have come.

CHAPTER 3

"This is going to sound really bad but... I have to leave you for a moment," David explains.

Camilla, naked in his arms, wonders why he must go so soon. They just had a great time, didn't they?

"But... where do you have to go?" she mumbles.

"I'm really enjoying our evening, but I didn't plan for it to play out like this. I was supposed to meet some friends."

She doesn't know how to take this and doubts start flooding in her mind. As if he could sense her distress, he caresses her face and presses his lips onto hers, still numb from his kisses.

"I'm happy," he whispers, his mouth gradually moving from her chin down to her neck, which he covers with little kisses, "I won't be long."

"What do you have to do that's so important?"

"I could tell you, but then I'd have to make sure you never tell anyone else," he coaxes, lying on top of her. He takes her face between his hands and kisses her softly. "I'll be quick," he promises before propping himself up.

She watches him get dressed, wondering where exactly he might be going with his friends. Any other man would have stayed with the girl in such conditions, but not him. Why?

"So,where are you going?"

"I'll share my secrets with you when our relationship is a bit more advanced. And I very much hope it'll happen."

No more questions. She is satisfied with his answer and she replies that she wants just the same. She decides to trust him. After all, it's not like he kicked her out of his apartment or anything. He'll be back.

After another kiss, he leaves.

Kraler watches the pretty blonde wiggle her hips against him. He knows exactly what she wants... which is the same thing as all the women who come to *Byzance*. This bar is a temple of debauchery. The police never ventures to this part of town. The south district is ruled by vampires.

He crushes his cigar butt in the ashtray. He only smokes socially. "Slash, go get us something to drink. I'm thirsty, and so is the lady," Kral roars.

His peer rises to his feet, ready to obey the instructions of his leader. And just like him, Slash is built like a tank. So much so that everybody moves away as he makes his way toward the counter. Feared by all, undoubtedly.

"Sit down," Kral barks at the blonde. She gives him a seductive look and complies. She had been trying to catch his attention for the past few evenings and decided to try her luck tonight. Kraler is very popular and being favored by him is an honor.

"Would you like to be alone with me?"

Not even the slightest smile appears on his face, which remains as cold and hard as a stone. Slash is back with their five whiskies and Kral knocks back his in a few seconds. "No," he finally replies.

Defeated, the young woman looks down at the ground.

"Dark, you can have fun with the lady."

The latter nods his head and motions for the girl to follow him.

"Any news regarding our matters, Friz?"

"No, Kral. Nothing new. Seems like the soldiers have finally come to their senses."

"Good for them."

His dark, stern face conveys fear and wickedness. And yet all their eyes are on him, hypnotized by his transcendental beauty. They would give anything for a glance, but none of them manages to catch his attention. He has but one simple objective: protect his species from the bastards that tried to exterminate it. They haven't crossed swords with him yet but when the time comes, he knows he will kill them all. He often resorts to force when his or his people's safety is at risk. That's how he got that impressive scar across his chest... he owes it to a hard-boiled opponent. He promised himself to find and eliminate him but he hadn't seen him again since their fight. He knows he is out there somewhere, lurking in the dark, waiting for any sign of weakness to pounce on him. Lately, he'd had to deal with young soldiers who were so inexperimented he had easily spotted them. According to Friz, they had stopped snooping around.

David joins his friends in a very isolated part of town. Nobody ever comes here, apart from mad people. Or suicidal people. It might be a good place to have a bit of inconsequential fun, but still, he doesn't understand these folks. Danger is everywhere, lurking.

The four men are walking towards *Byzance,* perfectly aware that the place if full of vampires – everybody knows – so why play with fire? Like every night, the bar is full of people David doesn't know. They are not wearing their military uniform as they are just here to check out the place and must absolutely pass unnoticed. The previous troop that was supposed to keep an eye on the leader had quickly been exposed.

No room for error.

They sit at a table, trying to blend in the crowd. Bastien goes to get drinks while they look around as if nothing was happening. Suddenly, David recognizes them. He can't be mistaken. The description was clear enough. There are four of them – seems like the fifth one is missing tonight – and they are all buff. One of them is blond and has a nasty spark in the eyes. Another one has long black hair, a scar across his face and exudes malice. There is also a brown-haired guy whose face breaks into a confident smile every time a pretty girl walks by their table. And then there is him: black hair, dark eyes, an eyebrow piercing and a stubble. The leader of the vampire clan. If the tattooed one wasn't missing, the whole *Snake* team would be present. The *Snakes.* That's what this group of vampires who rule this part of Seattle and fight for the protection of their species call themselves.

Bastien is back with their drinks and notices the clan. They have been in the military for a few years and their secret mission is to exterminate the rebellious vampires... but as long as they are under the protection of the Snakes, they know things won't be easy. However, once their leaders are down, they will be able to kill the rest of all those blood-thirsty monsters. Their respective species could have co-existed but some vampires attack humans and more particularly pretty young women. The lucky ones get their memories erased after being attacked, the not-so-lucky ones are just left behind to die in the street.

David and his group were given the mission to exterminate the unruly creatures. First, they need to locate the place and the predators, then they can take action.

Kraler glances at his watch.11:45 PM. "Let's go," he decides.

The clan gets up as one man and exits *Byzance* under the soliders' eyes. After a few steps in the street, the Snakes exchange looks. Kraler can sense the damn human soldiers. They haven't given up yet. The four men grab their guns and turn around at the same time to direct their weapons at four incompetents. Kraler sensed their presence. They all did. They are those who have been following them for weeks. Although they seem very young, the group leader doesn't have a single hesitation. He won't let them run now that he's got hold of them.

"Shoot!"

The order is given. The Snakes riddle their enemies with bullets in the middle of the street. It is dark outside and the streets are nearly deserted. Only a few party-goers are walking in and out of the club. The soldiers collapse onto the sidewalk, coloring it dark red as Kral and the others store their firearms.

Alerted by the gunshots, David, Kevin, Bastien and Alan hurry out of the bar and assess the awful display. David lifts up his eyes and sees the vampires walk away. "Monsters!" he growls, his fists clenched.

Alan calls the base to report the deaths of the young recruits. The lads hadn't been following the vampires these past few days as they knew they were exposed, but they had decided to resume work tonight because they had heard that an important meeting was supposed to take place between the Snakes and an unprincipled geneticist. They had told David, who had advised them against it, but they had decided to go anyway.

His fists are tightly clenched and his eyes are full of burning tears as he watches the clan disappear. He promises himself to kill every last one of them.

CHAPTER 4

It is 7 PM when Camilla, who is in a particularly good mood today, joins Angel at the terrace of a lovely little restaurant. She spent the night with David, even though he disappeared God-knows-where for two hours. Even before talking about the menu, she tells her friend about their dawning relationship.

"I'm happy for you," Angel grins.

Camilla keeps talking about the young man during the whole meal before finally realizing that Angel is too quiet and reserved compared to her normal self.

"What's going on, Angel?"

Angel nods her head, and Camilla understands that she probably hasn't been listening to her for a while. "Does it have something to do with you trying to call me yesterday?"

"..."

"Angel!"

"Sorry."

"What's going on?"

"I went back to *Byzance*, yesterday."

"Did you see him?"

"I did see him, but he didn't see me. I'm invisible to him," Angel fulminates.

She then sets about telling Camilla all the details about her evening at the bar, which makes her feel a little guilty as she barely paid any attention when her friend was telling her about her date.

"You know what I think? I think you should never set foot in that bar again."

Camilla is right. Kral is not a good person, he gives off something terrifying. He could be a contract killer... he certainly looks like one. Even worse, he could be a serial killer wanted in several countries.

"We didn't use any protection."

"The best thing to do is to make sure you didn't get any STDs."

Angel agrees, but in order to do that, she needs to see him again and ask him the question. She smiles, happy to have a good excuse to approach him.

"I should probably ask him."

"Uh, no. You should go and have a blood test."

It may sound like a logical and sensible suggestion but Angel's brain tends to shut off as soon as she thinks about Kral and it is her heart and desire to see him again that take over. She is then incapable of thinking straight as the only thought in her mind is: *go and see him.*

Camilla seems oblivious to her friend's internal turmoil. She wishes her a good evening before setting off for another date with David. He is taking her to see a movie tonight. Angel watches her as she leaves. Her friend looks very happy, and she is sure that her relationship with David will work perfectly. Camilla's past love life hadn't been very successful. The last boyfriend she had was always on her back and didn't respect her private space. The one before was pathologically jealous. David seems normal. At least in comparison with her *heart* sister's exes.

When the moon shines bright in the sky, Angel pushes the door of Byzance. This time, she doesn't need to make up excuses. She knows why she is there. She sits directly at the counter as her eyes scan the room. Stephan isn't there and another barman asks her what she would like to drink. She chooses a hard liquor, which she downs in one single gulp. After paying for the drink, she begins to look for Kral. Seems like he isn't there. Fine. She doesn't mind waiting.

One hour later, her patience is rewarded. Kral appears surrounded by his gang. They sit down at their usual table. She notices a man with black hair and tattoos whom she hadn't seen before. A new friend? Who cares! The guy who calls himself Friz gets up and orders some drinks at the counter. Nothing is attractive about him and he looks as frightening as the rest of them. Only Kraler is scary in a sexy kind of way. She can't explain it but she certainly isn't the only one who feels that way... most of the women start hovering around him as soon as he walks into the bar.

As Friz returns to his seat, Angel downs another drink before making her way towards their table. Her mind is blank and it is probably better that way, otherwise she would already be turning around, ready to run for her life. She stands in front of Kraler, praying not to lose her self-control. The last thing she wants is to look like an idiot again.

"Can we talk for a sec?" she asks and congratulates herself on not stammering.

Kral's eyes fall on her and he looks at her from head to toes without saying anything. The silence makes her uncomfortable. The four other men are also staring at her and she would like to disappear.

"You're looking tense, Kral. You should ask her to help you relax before agreeing to listen to what she has to say."

Angel turns her head in the direction of the guy who just spoke. What a jerk. She'd slap him in the face if she had the guts. Him too, seems to take her for some kind of promiscuous girl.

"Yeah... why not!"

Kral nods his head. But who is he talking to? Clearly not to his friend. He's speaking to her. She isn't entirely sure but he rises to his feet unsteadily, looking tired or *tense* – as the other guy would put it. She feels tiny as he towers above her. He's at least 10 inches taller than her.

"Come here."

She tags after Kral as he walks towards the counter, climbs up the four steps and then follows him into what looks like an office. He sits down in a big black leather armchair.

"We're not going to get in trouble?"

"It's my office. I own the club."

Ah! She had no idea. Now that she thinks about it, she doesn't remember ever seeing him pay for his drinks.

"Kneel down!"

He spreads his legs and starts undoing his belt buckle. Well, now she's got the answer to her question. He was obviously talking to his friend when he said *why not*.

"No!"

His eyes dart to her. He thought that was what she wanted. He may not think highly of women, but that is mostly because he has never been in love and because all the girls he has ever met are only interested in the prestige that comes with being seen with him. The women who know him well and are aware of his position in the social hierarchy want to strut about holding his hand and try to convince him to regain his status – the one he refused more than once.

"I'm not that kind of girl!"

"You'd be the first one. Didn't I bang you the other day?"

How rude! She can't believe it. Their relationship is nothing else but physical! What did she expect anyway? She must *not* let him confuse her.

21

"Is that a question or an affirmation?"

He chuckles. Her heart pounds in her chest as she watches him. It is the first time she sees him laugh and she finds him even more divinely handsome. He should definitely smile more often. He doesn't look scary anymore but almost human.

"It's definitely an affirmation."

She feels relieved. She almost thought he had forgotten. Now that she feels comfortable in his presence, she doesn't want to get his back up again.

"It seems that you're a bit tense." She places her hands over his broad shoulders but his thick black leather coat is in the way. "Would you like to take this off?"

He complies. She can now massage the giant's strained muscles. The word *tense* is hardly strong enough.

"My name is Angel."

"Kraler."

"I know."

She keeps on rubbing his back. Her fingers appease him. He relaxes and lets go of the stress that eats him up every day. The problem is, she finds it hard to focus only on his neck and shoulders when all she really wants is for him to pull her close and... She is hot now and cannot touch him without feeling compelled to take it further.

"Please don't stop... it feels so good."

Her heart beats faster. Why must he say that? He's totally torturing her! She puts her hands back on his shoulders but can't stand it more than a few minutes. The reason of her presence in this room strikes her suddenly and makes her lose concentration. She mentally slaps herself.

"I..."

It's so difficult to focus she loses her composure and her voice at the same time. The effect he has on her... it's poisonous and uncontrollable.

"We didn't..."

His hands suddenly grab hers. He pulls her in front of him and she feels herself melting completely. "What were you saying?" He doesn't let go of her. He could. At least that way she wouldn't be so tense, but he seems like... well, she doesn't really know, it's hard to tell. He doesn't look like he is taking perverse pleasure in touching her like he does, just simple, genuine pleasure.

"... use any protection."

"You won't risk anything with me."

She doesn't know why, but she believes every word he says. His eyes are hypnotizing. The man she is facing doesn't seem like his usual self. It is as if he could convince her of anything just by looking at her, which is very unsettling.

"Can you massage my back for a few more minutes?"

She gladly accepts and he lets go of her so she can resume her position behind him and grant his request. No words are exchanged as Angel's hands massage the giant's muscles, but the silence is comforting. She may have seen him as a crude man before but her image of him is starting to change.

Kraler is enjoying this relaxing treat. He is constantly busy and stressed. Plus, the girl seems to know what she's doing, and she does it very well. After a few minutes, he grasps one of her soothing hands and uses it to pull her in front of him so he can have a good look at her. He has never really looked at her before but he willingly admits that she is beautiful. He runs a hand through her long black hair and meets her emerald eyes. She doesn't look anything like the local women dying to get their hands on him. He doesn't know where she lives, but she is definitely not from around here. What is she doing in a bar like this? She certainly doesn't look like a wild party-goer, she must have just wanted to check out the place and see what is was like. But she came back. It's impossible for a girl like her to enjoy this kind of ambiance, diametrically opposed to what she gives off. Then what?

She came back for me.

The conclusion seems obvious yet completely absurd. No woman had ever been *sincerely* interested in him. What they were truly attracted to was his prestigious status.

A military spy? Possible. Why would such a beautiful woman be after a blood-thirsty monster like him if she didn't have a good reason? He must find out, and he is even surprised that the question didn't cross his mind before.

"What did you want from me?" His tone isn't as friendly as it was a minute ago when he was still touching her. The cold, distant creature is back.

"I told you. I wanted to talk to you about what happened. I was worried about the fact that we didn't use any protection."

"Why are you here?"

"Here?" The uneasiness is back, although she felt perfectly comfortable two minutes earlier. He is even starting to scare her a little.

"Don't give me that crap! Girls like you don't hang out in places like *Byzance*. So, why are you here?" he insists.

She feels just the way she did when she spillt her beer all over him that first night.

"I heard about the place and I..."

"And you wanted to check it out. Ok. What now?"

He stares at her with that predatory look he often has, waiting for an answer. She feels frightened.

"I want to go home," she says before swallowing the lump in her throat. If looks could kill...

"Why are you after me?" His calm tone only makes him more terrifying. "You know who I am, don't you? And you came to kill me."

"To kill you? Of course not!"

She doesn't understand a word he is saying. Who is he? Kraler, the owner of *Byzance*. Why would she want to kill him?

"Are you really going to tell me you came back here just to see my pretty face?"

His voice is now loud and threatening. She swallows with difficulty. She is going to have to answer him and tell him the truth. Or else... She would rather not think about it. A shiver runs down her spine. What if he really is a killer?

"Come on, Angel! Did the cat eat your tongue?"

She is scared to death and seething with rage (but mostly scared to death) and he... makes fun of her? She can't just tell him why she came back and let him know how he makes her feel. It would sound completely ridiculous.

"Are you going to kill me?"

She could have found something better to say. *Yes, I could have.*

"That's an idea. At least I wouldn't have to worry about letting some spy get away."

"A spy? Who the hell are you and why are you so afraid of me?"

"Not afraid of you. Of what you might be."

"Well, I'm nobody."

He glares at her and his piercing, ice-cold eyes make her shiver. She just wants do disappear.

"The soldiers sent you here?"

"The soldiers?"

He got into trouble with the army? But what kind of trouble exactly? He must definitely be a serial killer who came here to hide.

"You have no idea what I'm talking about, do you?"

I might actually do. But she would like to understand. Especially now that his expression is softer. "You can talk to me."

He stares at her. Maybe. Maybe not. In any case, that's a very strange thing to say. Him, talk to some stranger? He isn't that stupid.

"So you really only came back to see me?"

"Yes."

He smiles despite himself. And Angel loves that grin.

24

"Do you want me to prove it to you?"

"How?"

She takes Kral's hand and places it on her heart. He can feel the fast beat of that organ he sometimes eats as a treat. She lets go of his hand but he leaves his on her chest and closes his eyes, focusing on the blood throbbing in her veins. His fangs are aching and slowly growing longer. He must now fight against the urge to drain the precious nectar out of her body. It would be so easy to sink his teeth into her delicate throat and suck all of her blood. His desire is strong and he usually yields to it without remorse. He never questions himself before taking action but this... this is different. He feels that it would be wrong so he stops touching her, spins around to face to desk and puts his tense hands flat on its cold surface.

"Go away."

The order is given in a surprisingly polite and calm tone. Angel doesn't want to leave now she was starting to feel like they were making progress. She gets closer to him and puts her hands on his hips to turn him around but he seems deeply rooted in the floor. She can see that he is battling against himself. But why? Does it have anything to do with her confession and what it might mean to him? If only he could love her too... but that just seems impossible.

Kraler's fangs hurt so much he won't be able to restrain himself much longer. His face is tense. If she sees him, she will understand. She will leave him alone. But is that really what he wants?

"Get the hell out of here!" he shouts at the top of his lungs, still as a statue.

Her hands jerk away from him. His tone isn't courteous anymore. It is cold and menacing. He scares her again. She ends up giving up and leaves the office, unable to figure out how to behave with him. How can he be so charming and smiling one moment and so cold and threatening the next? Despite all this, she knows she cannot fight her feelings, which only seem to become more and more overwhelming.

As Kraler finally turns around, he is relieved to see that she is gone. His face relax, his fangs retract and the pain fades away. That was close. Why does he even want to protect her anyway? Something is seriously wrong with him tonight. He rubs his chin with his hand, trying to collect his thoughts. She managed to help him relax but now the pressure is back on his shoulders!

CHAPTER 5

After spending the whole Sunday at home, Angel feels the urge to let go of the tension and decides to take a shower. She can't stop thinking about Kraler and what happened the day before. It had started so well! How dare he kick her out like he did? He was cold and menacing. Shivers run down her spine every time she thinks about it. How can he change his attitude from charming to terrifying in one flutter of lashes.

As she gets out of the shower, she wraps a towel around her damp body and casts a mechanical glance through the kitchen window. He is there. In the darkness. A tall, dark figure wearing a long black coat. She gets closer to the window just to make sure she isn't dreaming. It's definitely him. Attracted like a magnet, she shuffles in the direction of the entrance door and opens it hurriedly. She couldn't care less about the fact that the only thing she has on is a towel and to be honest, the thought doesn't even cross her mind. Their eyes lock. He is only a few steps away. There, on the other side of the road. Her heart pounds in her chest. Why did he come here? She hasn't got the slightest idea.

He followed her last night after she got out of *Byzance*. He followed her because her blood obsessed him, because he wanted to know where he could find her when he wouldn't be able to restrain himself anymore, when he would give in to the urge of... drinking her blood. He is now only a few feet away from her delicious smell. He inhales it, breathes it. There is something spicy and floral in her blood. It is probably exquisite, but that isn't what he came for. He even took the precaution to suck the vital energy out of a young human girl before coming here. To see *her*. He didn't plan for her to see him and let alone open her door. He intended to lurk in the dark and wait. But for what? He doesn't know. He starts approaches the house and Angel doesn't move. He walks in, pushing her back inside at the same time. He could have her now. It would be so easy. He will do it, but not like this. He is here because she obsesses him. He is intrigued by her attitude. No woman has ever shown such interest in him.

He embraces her slim figure before pressing her against him. The next second, he kisses her passionately. Damn it! He can't help it, she makes him lose control. Her towel falls onto the floor and he takes her upstairs to her room.

"Give yourself to me," he whispers in her ear, lying down beside her on the bed.

Angel is shaking with pleasure. She is incapable of thinking straight, like each time they are together. All she wants to do is give him what he desires. What he came looking for. Her.

Kraler takes his clothes off quickly and lies down next to her to caress her body. He finds her absolutely perfect and notes that she is having trouble breathing normally.

"Relax..." he murmurs.

"I love you," she stammers and immediately regrets these words. What is he going to think about her? The lamp in the living room casts a dim light into the bedroom, giving it a romantic atmosphere. She lets him caress her body with his huge warm hands and starts touching him as well, her fingers trailing across the scar on his chest.

"What is this?"

"A battle that could have cost me my life," he replies before imprisoning her hand in his.

He brings her fingers to his face and slides one into his mouth, sucking on it gently before letting go of her hand to kiss her. It is a long and stimulating for Angel who can feel her desire increasing. The next moment, Kraler's fingers are inside her. He is soft and incredibly gentle. So different from their first time. He doesn't seem like the same person. And yet...

After driving her insane with a few more burning strokes, he finally penetrates her with his manhood and hears her moan as their bodies fuse. He likes the sound of her voice and the way she arches her back to receive him. He wants her to abandon herself completely, and that is exactly what she does as he starts thrusting in and out of her. She lets him take possession of her body, her heart and soul, moaning as he quickly pulls out and slides his tongue into the most intimate part of her anatomy. He tastes her like he wanted to, giving her intense pleasure. He doesn't think about her blood one single moment even though he can hear her heartbeat and the sound of the hot liquid running through her veins. It is the elixir of life. Of her life. From that moment, he knows he will never take it from her. On the contrary, he will fight to protect it even if it means endangering his own life. He doesn't want to label what is happening between them or the way he feels about her, but she is important in a way no woman has ever been to him.

He savors the taste of her juices a bit longer before going back on top of her to resume his pounding. Finally, he comes deep inside her with one last, hard thrust. Sweating, he withdraws and lies down against her boiling skin. His smell is all over him now.

"I enjoyed making love to you, and I want to do it again," he says, leaning on his elbows to look at her and sweep a strand of hair off her face.

"Uhm... yes," she mumbles. She cannot believe what is happening. The man she found terrifying the previous day just made her climax as she never had before, and he wants to do it again.

"Now?" she ventures, and he smiles.

"Do you want to do it again now?"

His tone is so soft and sweet. Nothing like the way he used to speak to her. Her face breaks into a smile and she shivers. He strokes her body as she gazes at him. This man is unbelievably handsome and attractive. What is he doing here, in her bed? The thought crosses her mind but only for a second before focusing her attention on him again.

"Well, you said..."

Her sentence is cut short as he seals her lips with a feverish kiss and makes sweet love to her a second time.

"I hope you enjoyed it," he says softly, stroking her stomach and fiddling with the piercing – a ball – on her belly button.

"Yes," she smiles.

"I enjoyed it too," he confesses, running his fingers along her face. "But I'm going to have to go," he adds without realizing just how much of a jerk he sounds.

"What do you mean? You're not staying?"

"I have something to do."

Something to do? Her eyes land on the alarm clock on her night table. It's almost midnight. What is it that he must do at such a late hour? And what is she for him anyway? What about the moment they shared together?

"I just wanted to see you," he admits, "I didn't think you would see me, let alone that we would... I was harsh on you last night."

He seems ill at ease and his words sound like a very clumsy apology.

"So what is it that you have to do?"

He can tell her anything he wants, all she can think about now is that secret thing he needs to do in the middle of the night.

"It's complicated."

"Is it a woman?" She hates herself for asking the question. It's not like she owns him! She doesn't have a right to be jealous, but she can't help it.

"No, of course not," he objects softly.

She honestly didn't think he could be so sweet. He is a very surprising man and she has some serious trouble understanding him.

"I could tell you but... I'm afraid you'll run away from me."

Anxiety washes over her as she starts thinking about what he might really be. A serial killer? A paid assassin? Definitely the kind of job you would do in the middle of the night.

"Do you kill people?"

It takes her all she has to ask him that question, but she needs to know. She doesn't want to end up in a plastic bag or drained out of her blood. He looks serious and uneasy. Did she guess right? She swallows.

"We can talk about it some other time, ok? I really have to go."

"Alright."

He keeps staring at her, sensing her doubts and dawning fear. He doesn't know what she has in mind, but she is probably far from the truth. He doesn't want to give her the wrong impression. Despite what they just shared, she now seems uncertain. He caresses her face and her throat and lingers on her beautiful breasts, feeling her heartbeat speed up under his touch.

"I really want to see you again."

So does she. Her face relaxes into a little smile. The man who made such passionate love to her cannot be a bad guy. It's impossible.

"Will you let me come back?"

"Yes."

"I'm going to be pretty busy in the next few days but how about Thursday or Friday?"

"Anytime you want."

His fingers brush lightly over her breasts and stomach. He likes her piercing and starts twirling his tongue around it, this simple contact driving her crazy with desire. Her centre of pleasure isn't very far down and she wants him. Again. He tickles her navel for a few more seconds before moving downward. He wants to leave her panting, with his smell and his love imprinted in her skin to wash away the doubts from her mind. He's going to have to get her addicted if he wants to build something with her. It's his only option. Otherwise, she will hate him and run away without ever turning back. He wouldn't survive then. Couldn't.

After granting her another orgasm, Kraler leaves and Angel finds herself alone in her bed. No question comes to haunt her. Exhausted, she falls asleep surrounded by his smell, the image of his face imprinted in her memory.

It was hard for Kraler to leave the house of that human girl who ruffles him more than he would like and now he is late. Loud music is pumping at *Byzance* and the Snakes are all present. Kral joins them quickly without bothering to explain why he is late. Nobody says anything anyway, he is the boss and he can do whatever he pleases. He waves at them and makes his way into his office. Their secret meeting starts as soon as the door is closed. Tonight's subject: the soldiers. After the murders that took place the other night, they know the military men will retaliate and probably even send another troop after them. They must be very careful.

CHAPTER 6

Angel spends an unpleasant Monday morning at work as she fell asleep quite late last night. She feels worn out and keeps making mistakes when typing the letters her boss gave her. She works as an executive assistant in a tax firm and she is known to be the fastest.

At 10 o'clock, she takes a break and joins Sally and Amanda, two of her colleagues, by the coffee machine.

"Hey Angeline. So how did you like *Byzance*?"

She had heard of the bar through them and that was why she had wanted to go and check it out in the first place.

"Yeah it's alright."

"What, that's it?"

"No, it was awesome!" she exclaims.

The girls giggle. They are both in their twenties and have only ever been to the pub once.

"Really?" Sally asks, surprised.

"I met a guy there," Angel confesses.

Sally and Amanda exchange a conniving glance before setting their eyes full of questions on Angeline. They had told her about the place in the only hope that she would go. Both girls are malicious and nobody in the firm likes them. Angel tries not to judge them precociously as she is wants to believe that they are good at heart.

"Are you sure he was a human?" Amanda wants to know.

What the heck is she talking about? Of course he is! What else could he be?

"As far as I know," she shrugs.

"Because you know, rumor has it..." Sally begins.

"What?"

"Oh come on, Angeline. Don't tell me you have no idea what people say about that nasty neighborhood," Amanda barks.

Well apparently no, she has no clue, but she doesn't really keep up with the news or goes out very often, just like her sister. So how would she know?

"What am I supposed to be aware of?"

"That the south area of Seattle isn't in the hands of humans anymore."

Angel rolls her eyes. That idiot is totally pulling her leg!

"It's true! Don't you ever read the newspaper, go on the Internet?" Amanda insists. "Everyone's talking about it."

"About what?"

"You find out by yourself."

Angel doesn't have time to go on the Internet and look up some bogus information. She's got much better to do. Kral, for example. She terribly misses him. She watches as Amanda strolls off with her cup of coffee in her hands and then stares at Sally. Maybe she'll let her in on the whole secret. But then again, she's not that interested.

"We went to *Byzance* last week because we wanted to see them with our own eyes," Sally finally tells.

"See who?"

"The vampires."

Angel chokes on her coffee and bursts out laughing. Sally starts laughing too, but it sounds more like a snort. The blonde girl is just making fun of her colleague's ignorance. She walks off, leaving Angel on her own.

Nonsense. Complete nonsense. Vampires! Who the hell are they kidding?

Angel laughs quietly while sipping her coffee, convinced that her friend is just messing around with her. Vampires are but a myth nurtured by literature and television. None of this is real. A shiver runs down her back as she imagines Dracula holding a beer between his claw-like hands. The only reference she has is a bit outdated as those creatures are now at the peak of their popularity, especially amongst young women, but Angel doesn't have any interest in that sort of thing. She couldn't care less about blood-thirsty creatures, as attractive as they may appear.

In short, she doesn't believe it to be anything else but pure fiction.

The thought doesn't leave her until Latiana Rabosa walks into the boss's office. The beautiful, fourty-something woman knows everything about everything and for good reason: she's a journalist.

"Hello Angeline."

"Hello Mrs Rabosa."

"Is Mr Heinchein available at the moment?"

"He's currently with a client. Do you mind waiting for a few minutes?"

She gestures to a beige leather armchair and the woman sits down.

"Would you like a cup of coffee?"

"Thank you Angeline, but I'm fine."

The secretary resumes her typing until her phone starts ringing. She grabs it instantaneously as the screen reads "Camilla".

"Camilla!" she beams after picking up. "I have so much to tell you."

"*Wow, that much?*"

"You'll never believe me. I saw him again."

"*You went back to Byzance?*"

"To *Byzance*? Yeah, on Saturday and yesterday he came to my house."

"*Do you have time for a drink after work?*"

"How about you come and have dinner at my place? That way we can talk."

"*Alright. I'll be there at 7.*"

"Can't wait."

She hangs up with a pretty smile on her face, impatient to tell her friend about what happened with Kral, the dark handsome owner of *Byzance*.

"Were you just talking about *Byzance*, the bar?" Mrs Rabosa asks her.

"Uhm, yes."

"You shouldn't go there. You're too pretty for your own good!"

"Uhm... why?"

"Don't you know that the owner of the place is a vampire?"

Her words feel like a slap in her face, a knife in her heart. A vampire? Kraler, a vampire?

"Vampires rule the south area," the journalist explains.

Angel is speechless, shocked, petrified. The door to her superior's office suddenly swings open and the handsome fifty-something man appears, followed by a much younger man. They shake hands and then Mr Heinchein focuses his attention on Mrs Rabosa.

"Come in, my dear," he welcomes her, gesturing to his office.

The mature woman glances at Angel before disappearing into the boss's office.

A vampire? Angel is still under the shock. She is incapable of thinking properly, as if that simple word had created a short-circuit in her brain and it needed time to assimilate the news.

Angel doesn't know how she survived the day and how she made it home. The only thing she knows is that she is completely lost and doesn't feel like doing anything, and she definitely doesn't want to think. Stretched out on the sofa, she tries to escape reality.

Kraler, a vampire.

It's impossible! She would have noticed something was wrong, and in any case, vampires don't even exist! It is pure invention! But why would Mrs Rabosa tell her such a stupid lie? She's a journalist, and a very famous one to boot. She knows her business, so it must be true. Angel tries to reason herself, but is it really her place to question what such an important woman told her? And if she accepts to believe that... aberration, she's going to have to deal with it, which seems pretty complicated.

How could she not guess it? Well, how could she have guessed it? How was she supposed to know that their species secretly co-exist with humans? There was no way she could have figured it out. Nothing could have led her to suspect such a thing. The question now is, what exactly is a vampire? The answer comes quickly: a human-looking creature who drinks blood from living beings. She jumps as the doorbell rings.

Kral? God, no!

She starts panicking, not wanting to see him just yet, before remembering that Camilla is supposed to come and have dinner with her and that she hasn't prepared anything. She rises to her feet and heads for the door.

"I haven't prepared anything," she sighs.

"It's okay, I feel like eating pizza anyway!"

Well, there is nothing to worry about, after all. Angel notices that Camilla is beaming with joy and concludes that it must be because of her love story with David.

"Do you have any leaflets?"

"Kraler is a vampire."

Camilla turns her head to stare at her friend. What the hell is she talking about?

"Who is Kraler?"

"You know, the guy I met at *Byzance*."

"Oh yeah, sorry. A vampire, are you sure?"

Angel tells her about Mrs Rabosa's warning after she overheard their conversation on the phone about *Byzance*, but also about Sally and Amanda's words, which now make total sense.

"So what's going on with you guys?"

"I'm talking about vampires... why aren't you calling me crazy?"

It isn't the reaction she was expecting. She would have wanted her friend to tell her that these creatures are purely fictional, that Kraler is definitely human

34

but the fact that Camilla doesn't say anything like that only confirm her sister's suspicions.

"Let me tell you something Angel. I know they're real. And I know what's happening in the south district."

"So why did you agree to go to *Byzance*?"

"Because I thought we didn't risk anything inside a crowded club. And nothing happened!"

"Of course not."

"Did you see him again?"

"He came by last night. He knows where I live."

The thought sends a wave of panic through her. Knowing that this blood drinker has her address terrifies her. He might show up at any moment, and it's obvious that if Kraler tries to attack her, she won't be strong enough to fight back.

"Relax, alright?" Camilla demands as she sees Angel turning pale.

"He's supposed to come back."

"When?"

"On Thursday or Friday."

"What do you guys do together?"

"What do you think?" she snarls, lifting her eyebrows. "I think I'm in love with that... thing."

"Don't overreact, ok? Maybe he's a good guy."

"How can you say that?"

Angel feels like the world has come to an end although Camilla doesn't seem particularly bothered. She knows about their species and she also knows that vampires have been co-existing with humans for decades. Most of them aren't even dangerous... most of them. This isn't news at all for her.

"Pizza with pepperoni, or do you want something else for a change?"

Her casual tone drives Angel insane. But maybe she's right, maybe she's just overreacting. It's not the end of the world after all. Being a vampire doesn't necessarily mean being bad. Kraler is far from looking like Dracula, but that doesn't mean she won't keep away from him.

"Yeah, alright," she answers in a sigh.

Why is she the only one shocked by reality? She tells her friend that she doesn't want to see Kraler anymore and Camilla doesn't really understand. Is she in love, yes or no? She warned her about him from the beginning, but who knows, there might be a good guy hiding behind his cold façade. Because she is so happy with David, her bias about the vampire is diminished. She's

35

usually better at judging people, but love tends to have that mellowing effect on her.

During the evening, Angels agrees to have a drink at *Byzance* with Camilla, David and his friends the next day. Thursday. At least she won't be home if Kraler decides to show up. She wants to keep away from him, move on and stop feeling sorry for herself. Now how is she going to tell him? She hopes he will understand when he realizes there is nobody at home, because she doesn't want to confront him. It might make her look like a coward, but she doesn't care. All the memories she has with him are painful. Now that she knows who he really is, she fears him even more. He scares her and she just wants to... forget him.

As if she could just bury her head in the sand!

CHAPTER 7

That very evening, Friz walks into *Byzance* with some good news for the Snakes: he managed to uncover the soliders who were after them. Everyone smiles. Kraler congratulates him and asks for their names but he knows none of them. It must be a new troop.

"Where can we find them? What do they look like?" Kral asks.

"That's them," Friz replies, handing out a photo of four men.

Kraler grabs the picture and gives it a good look before passing it to Slash, who then passes it to the person next to him.

"We can find them in a club downtown. They don't go there very often, but we could corner them there."

"Good," Kral smiles, "Let's go now." He can't wait to get there and be done with it. It would so much easier if the military would stop sending soldiers after them, but he knows how to get rid of them. And if needed, he will even blow up the nearest base. They had discussed it before and it wouldn't be much of a hassle. A piece of cake.

It isn't long before the Snakes arrive at *Retro*, the most popular, central club. Only humans here, not a single vampire. All eyes are on them as they walk in and sit down at a table. Their unusual style gets people whispering amongst them. They don't really blend in with the others but that doesn't really matter according to Kral and his men. The only thing that matters is the soldiers.

Viper beckons a sexy waitress as she strolls by their table and orders some drinks. The poor girl looks scared to death as her eyes dart from one giant to another.

"Can't see any soldiers in here," Dark observes.

"It's not even 11PM yet. Give'em some time," Slash retorts.

The young waitress comes back with their drinks and Kral pays for them, which isn't something he is used to doing. He usually only goes to *Byzance*, which he owns. They spend the evening drinking and waiting but no soldier shows up. They have to face reality, it's a lost cause. The group decides to come back the next day and leaves.

Kraler hated that night wasting their time. Even more so because they will need to come back every day until the soldiers decide to show up. He will waste a lot of time when he could have spent it with Angel. He had planned to see her on Thursday or Friday... but he will not be able to wait that long. His body wants her. How can he be so addicted to a woman who isn't even a vampire?

On Thursday, Kraler is in a terrible mood as he knows he is going to waste yet another night waiting for the soldiers. Spending the evening with Angel sounds much more tempting, even though he can't explain it or give it some kind of particular meaning.

"Ready, boss?" Slash asks.

"I hate that stupid club and those stupid soldiers!"

Slash reveals a devilish smile. "We can go and do the deed without you if you want." He can't wait for the confrontation, he sure is going to have some fun with the soldiers, as opposed to his friend, who doesn't seem as interested or excited as usual. Something is definitely going on with him, but trying to get Kral to talk about his problems is like trying to get a fish to moonwalk. "They'll regret ever crossing my path, I can assure you."

Kraler exits *Byzance*, impatient to get this over with. He hopes that they will show up quickly so they can move on and he can go and see Angel. He needs to hold her close, taste her and possess her. His shaft hardens just thinking about her. He forces the thought out of his head. He needs to focus.

"We're following you!" Slash laughs.

The Snakes fall into step behind their leader.

The girls walk into *Retro* where David and his friends are waiting for them. Camilla shares a passionate kiss with David while Angel timidly waves at everybody.

"What would you like to drink, ladies?" Kevin asks, gazing at both of them. The first one looks a bit lost while the second one is imprisoned in his friend's arms. "Come on David, let her breathe!" he laughs, and everybody follows. David finally releases the young woman from his embrace.

"So, what shall I order?" Kevin reiterates.

"Angel and I will have Desperados," Camilla answers, looking at her friend.

Angeline nods in agreement. She shouldn't have come. She should have stayed home, cradled in her bed, and if Kral had showed up she just wouldn't have opened the door for him.

Kevin heads for the counter while David starts kissing Camilla again. Great! Angel can already picture them morphing into one single being with two heads and four arms. Oh, loneliness. Seeing them together hurts her, makes her think about Kraler and it is the least thing she wants.

Kevin is back with their two bottles, which he puts down onto the table. The girls usually drink in glasses but tonight, Angel doesn't seem to mind drinking from the bottle. Her mind is elsewhere and she feels like an outcast.

"Wow, you were thirsty!"

"Yeah," she smiles politely.

"So, what's up?" Camilla asks before grabbing her bottle. She glances at everybody, not speaking to anybody in particular.

Kevin answers her question, telling her about his week. Bastien and Alan talk together while David covers Camilla's throat with little kisses.

Angel feels more and more lonely. She lifts the beer to her lips and drinks a few sips, thinking that she never should have agreed to come. She should have stood up for herself and confronted reality and Kraler. A vampire. She can't help but think about him, about the fact that she made love with a blood drinker, that she gave him her body, her heart and soul. The only thing he didn't take from her was her blood. Maybe that's why he's so interested in her. He's looking for something to eat. She swallows at the thought and drinks a few more gulps from her beer. After a few more bottles, Angel starts to feel less bored and more relaxed.

Camilla is a bit less focused on David and give her a bit more attention. "Have you heared from your boyfriend?"

"Boyfriend?" Angel sighs. Kraler is NOT her boyfriend.

"Oh, you have a boyfriend?" Kevin butts in.

Last thing they need is for Camilla to tell everybody that Kral is a vampire. They'd all run for their lives! Or they would call her crazy and throw garlic at her. "It's over," she replies.

"Not necessarily," Camilla retorts.

39

Angel lets out a sigh. Her sister perfectly knows who he is and why she shouldn't see him again. That's why Angel agreed to spend the night with them in the first place!

"Of course it is!"

"What's the story?" David wants to know.

"It's not important," Angel interrupts before Camilla gets a chance to open her mouth.

"We're guys, you could have a masculine point of view," Alan suggests.

She can tell they won't let it drop and it is exactly the sort of conversation she doesn't want to have. But if she refuses to speak, Camilla might do it for her, so she finally tells, "He's been hiding things from me, that's all."

"Like what?"

God, they're so curious! "Things about himself."

"That's pretty vague."

"I don't want to talk about it anyway."

"As you wish."

Really? She didn't think it would be this easy. She expected to be harrassed with questions. She feels glad and relieved for sure. "Camilla, will you come with me to the bathroom?"

Her friend agrees and once they are alone in the ladies' room, Angel tells her that she doesn't want her to tell them any more details about her love story with the vampire.

The Snakes shoot a quick glance through the window. The soldiers are inside the club.

"Alright!" Slash rubs his hands together. He can hardly wait for the battle. "Shall we just rush in?"

"We're not in our territory here," Dark tempers.

"He's right," Kraler agrees, "We can't just wreak bloody havoc in front of all these humans."

"We could wait for them to get out," Friz suggests.

"That's exactly what we're going to do," Kral decides, "Let's get in and sit at the other end of the room."

Heads turn as the Snakes walk into the club. Once again, their rebellious look does not go unnoticed.

"Damn... I wanted to blend in with the crowd. Totally failed," Kral says as they sit down.

From where they are seated, they can keep an eye on the soldiers but the military men can't see them. All they have to do now is wait. But something troubles Kral. A smell. A familiar smell.

It is her.

It seems impossible, but he knows she is here and he needs to see her, the urge is stronger than him.

"What would you like to drink?" asks a waitress.

"Five beers," Viper replies.

She walks away as he looks her up and down greedily. She is perched on high heels, her legs are long and slip and she is wearing a revealing miniskirt and plunging top. *She's hot!* "Yummy!"

"Enough, Viper. This isn't our territory," Friz grumbles.

"I know that for God's sake! You've been repeating it over and over again since we got here."

"You're damn right we have! This is the soldiers' territory."

"Chill the fuck out, I'm not going to eat the bitch!

"Viper! Kral, tell him to shut the hell up."

But their leader is in his own little world, obsessed by the familiar flavor he cherishes. He needs to find her. Now.

"Kral?"

The waitress puts their drink on their table and Friz gives her the money as Kral seems completely out of it. "What's up?" he asks the others.

"He must be thinking," Dark assumes.

"Or maybe he's daydreaming," Slash snorts. He elbows Kral, bringing him back to reality.

"What?"

"You're not with us."

"I was just thinking." Kral grabs his bottle and gulps down hal of his beer. He can't seem to get Angel out of his head, which is a very toxic thing given the circumstances. She shouldn't even be here. He must find her and tell her to leave, so he starts scanning the room, looking for her.

"Something wrong?" Dark asks.

"I don't know yet... but..."

Oh no! He can't talk about some human girl. None of them would understand. He doesn't even understand it himself.

"Kral, check that out. Isn't that the girl who wanted to talk to you the other night?" Viper cries.

Kraler's eyes fall on the girl. She has long dark hair and is simply beautiful. His body wants her more than ever since he smellt her perfume. Angel. She is

41

with a brunette he doesn't know. A friend, perhaps. "Yeah," he says, "That's her."

"Did she give you head that one time?"

If Viper had been talking about any other girl, Kral wouldn't have cared. He might have even laughed before giving him some details, but not this time. He is talking about Angel. He tears his gaze off the beautiful young woman and fixes it on his friend. But the latter can't see it as he is still staring at Angel.

"Damn it Kral! Look at that! What a bitch!"

Everyone turns their gaze on her as she and her friend sit down at a table where four other men are seated. The soldiers. Kral rubs his chin. *God damnit!*

"What do we do? They might be in the military too," Friz ponders.

"Such a bitch. That's why she was after me," Kral whispers. The thought had left him but now he is convinced that it is the reason why she ever showed any interest towards him. He was wrong, and now he has the evidence. She pretended to be interested in him and he was starting to... what a piece of trash! He is determined to end this battle and once he is done with her, she will regret ever crossing his path.

"Mission canceled," the leader snarls, "Find everything you can about those girls."

Boiling with rage, he gets on his feet and heads for the exit, the rest of the gang on his heels.

CHAPTER 8

Angel gets back home after spending the night drinking and chatting. She might have been bored in the beginning, but she ended up having fun with the others. She stayed as late as possible, hoping that Kral would come during her absence and find an empty house. He had better never come back. She is pretty sure he won't show up again; it is 3AM. It might not be very safe to walk home by herself at such a late hour, but she doesn't live very far from *Retro*.

She can see her house. What a relief! She quickens her step, then stops abruptly. He didn't get the message. He is there. Kraler is sitting on her porch, waiting for her. She swallows. It is dark, she is alone and a vampire is sitting in front of her. Sounds like the scenario of a horror movie.

Kraler lifts his eyes to look at her as soon as he senses her presence. They are dark and menacing, completely different from those she remembers from that night he came to see her. He now feels nothing but digust toward the woman who wronged him. He stares at her for a moment, sensing her fear. The poor girl doesn't know what she's in for. She doesn't know how he is when somebody betrays him. Kraler is a man of honor and does not go along with error, manipulation or lies.

He rises to his feet, his threatening gaze still fixed on her. "We need to talk!" Every word is pronounced distinctly and his request sounds more like an order.

Angel swallows her saliva before taking a few steps to open the entrance door. She walks in and he follows behind. He has an intimidating and imposing demeanor that scares her to death. The only thing she doesn't understand is why he is acting that way. Unless... Of course. He came in this evening, noticed that she wasn't there and started imagining things. All the time he spent waiting must have driven him crazy. Now she's going to have to find a way to calm him down. She swallows again.

"What are you playing at?" His tone is harsh, as she expected. He probably doesn't understand what happened and she will have to explain everything. She tries and pluck up her courage. Why is it so hard?

"You thought I wouldn't find out!" he yells, slamming his fist on the table.

She jumps and sobers up instantly. All the alcohol evaporates from her blood. Fortunately, the table is between them but she is convinced he could throw it against the wall if he wanted to.

"I'm sorry," she mumbles. She feels terrible for not finding something better to say but stringing two words together while facing such a muscular giant is quite difficult, not to say impossible.

"Sorry? Are you kidding me?" He hits the table one more time before putting his hands flat on its surface, his gaze riveted on her. And what a dark gaze! It might be the right moment to tell him she knows about his true nature. She would like for him to soften a bit so they can talk.

"I know who you are."

"Of course you do," he says and takes his hands off the table. He straightens up and starts pacing around the room. He wants to calm down so she can tell him, explain him, and then he will make her regret what she did.

She stares at him, powerless and shaking. He could wipe the floor with her!

"I thought that if I didn't stay at home tonight, you would understand that I do not want to see you again." She managed to speak without stammering. Good. The vampire spins around briskly and stares into her eyes without saying a word, giving her the impression that he can see through her and search her mind, which makes her feel uncomfortable.

"What did you do tonight, then?" His voice is a bit calmer and Angel relaxes ever so slightly. Perhaps he will soften and they will be able to talk.

"I was out with friends."

"Friends, right?"

Why does he sound so sarcastic? Does he think that she has no friends? That she's some kind of antisocial outcast?

"That's right. With Camilla, her boyfriend and his pals." *Who does he think he is?* He doesn't have the right to question what she says or interrogate her like this. She wants him out of the house. She just wants to go to sleep. Well, it's not like she could fall asleep anyway.

Kraler hates that she keeps on lying, it drives him even more insane. Who is she? What does she want? He wants to know so he can spit it back in her face. She doesn't deserve any sympathy or special treatment. Nothing. He is going to worm it out of her, torture her if he needs to, but she is going to talk.

She must tell her everything she knows. Only then, he will drain her blood out and end her.

"Listen to me carefully," he orders, "I know who you are and why you wormed your way into my life. What I don't know is what you were looking for, so you're going to tell me now."

"I didn't worm my way into your life, and we've already had this conversation."

"I remember." He starts pacing in the kitchen. There isn't a lot of space and he can't bear being confined in such a narrow place. He needs to move, to do something. "But you lied to me!" He leaps in front of her and meets her gaze. Why does she have to be so beautiful and ignite such impulses from him? He should probably keep his distance, but he can't seem to move backward.

"I... did not... lie," she articulates slowly.

"I don't want to play tag!" he roars, "I don't have time for this. I saw you with your friends!" He moves away from her and reaches the other side of the table. That way he can keep a clear mind.

"So what?"

"What do you mean 'so what'? I didn't like seeing you there!"

"I stood you up. Get over it!"

Her anger brings a smile to his face. "I couldn't care less about that, I'm talking about your position in the army!" His clenched fists slam hard on the table as he says that, causing it to break under the shock. Angel steps backward until she is pressed against the wall. He is completely beside himself and she is terrified. So much for trying to act like a brave girl!

"What do you have to say to that?" he yells again and she can feel her eyes tearing up. If he lost control one single moment... she could be dead. He would murder her. "I'm waiting!"

He's waiting? Waiting! She doesn't even remember what he said. The only thing she recalls is her table breaking in half. What incredible strength! She can't even imagine what his fists could do to her if he decided to hit her. She would break in half, too.

"What were you hoping to do by getting close to me?" he badgers her, and she can't find anything to reply. She is terrified and there is a knot in her throat. She is standing in front of a deadly vampire! Anyone in the same situation would react like her.

"For fuck's sake! Will you open your damn mouth?"

"I... I want you to leave." It took her all she had to say these words. No pride in that though, her eyes are burning and she is still fighting against the tears she doesn't want this monster to see.

"I won't leave until I've heard the whole story. I want answers and you're going to give them to me!"

She doesn't even know what the hell he's talking about! She doesn't understand a word he says. She can't ask him though, because she will undoubtedly start crying if she opens her mouth.

Kral sits down on a chair, folds his arms across his chest and stares at her. "I don't mind waiting." He doesn't seem to see how much she is hurt and scared. Angel lets go of the tension and her body slides down against the wall until she is sitting down on the tiled floor. She wraps her arms around her legs and puts her head on her knees. She looks away from that barbarian she dreads, praying that he will disappear, even though it seems very unlikely.

"I wanted to keep away from you because I found out who you really are," she finally explains.

He observes her, thinking. His stare seems to soften until the heartless warrior mask he was wearing drops. "And what am I, exactly?" His tone isn't authoritative anymore but calm and courteous.

"A vampire." The word dies between her lips, but he hears it perfectly because of his extraordinary ears.

"How did you find out?"

"A journalist who heard me talk about *Byzance* told me at work."

"You are a journalist?"

"No, an executive assistant. She had an appointment with my boss." She manages to look at him without bursting in tears or feeling afraid. Kraler is back to being the charming man he was with her a few days ago.

"What were you doing with the exterminators?"

"I have no idea what you're talking about. What the hell is an exterminator?"

His eyes are riveted on her. She looks weak and exhausted, less scared and finally open to discussion. Maybe it was a good idea to get so worked up after all.

"A soldier," he answers calmly.

"What does that have to do with me?"

"They have it against my community."

"Vampire exterminators," she understands.

"Yes. And you were with them."

"When?"

She lifts up her head to look at him properly. Now what is he on about?

"Tonight."

"That's impossible!" she objects furiously, "I was with Camilla and..." *Vampire exterminators?* It doesn't make sense! She would have known. Everything is coming down on her!

"You didn't know," he murmurs. He just realized. How stupid of him to accuse her like that! And what an idiot he was to show up here like a madman ! He pulls a black wallet out from his trench coat pocket and takes a wad of bills out before placing them onto the work surface of the kitchen. "There enough here for you to buy a new table... I'm really sorry."

It is the first time he apologizes to a woman. To anybody, for that matter. He is ready to admit his mistakes but he had never stooped so low for a girl before. The next moment, he walks out of the house with incredible speed.

CHAPTER 9

Kraler tries to blend in with the dark. How stupid is he and also, why is he so good at doing stupid things? He hates himself for that but it's too late. He should have believed her from the beginning, or at least give her the benefit of the doubt. Now she's never going to want to see him again and the thought is enough to enrage him. She just found out about his true nature and he wasn't even able to reassure her. He was completely blinded by his anger until he realized she was sincere. She knows nothing about the soldiers.

He walks through the south disctrict of Seattle without any particular goal but to evacuate the rage still boiling inside of him. He needs to calm down and then he can start thinking.

"Hey, handsome!"

He stops and spins on his heels to face a beautiful creature. He looks at her for a moment. A brunette with a long wavy mane and a short dress. A prostitute, obviously.

"How much are you ready to pay to spend a moment with me?"

Her question confirms his first impression. Would sex help him relax? She is very pretty indeed, and usually she could have distracted him for a few hours, but his frustration stands in the way of his desire.

"Come on honey, there's an alley right over there."

He shots a glance in the direction she is indicating. It is very dark and there isn't a single street lamp. It does look like the ideal place to abandon oneself to all kinds of fantasies. He nods his head and the prostitute leads him towards the alley, behind a garbage container. She lifts up her dress quickly but he interrupts her. It is not lust but hunger that takes over and he pounces on her like a predator and wraps his hand around her neck before sinking his fangs into her soft skin. Hot blood is what he desires. Stealing somebody's life is an immense satisfaction as well as a perfect way to relax. Kraler does not belong to this group of vampires who co-exist with humans and drink blood from animals or artificial blood. He wants human blood. He needs it to stay strong and fit. If he made the same choice as some of his peers, he wouldn't be able to fight the soldiers anymore, let alone defeat them. The Snakes need to drink from the source, and that is exactly what the soldiers – and probably Angel – reproach them for.

After drawing the life out of her, he leaves her unconscious on the ground. She will probably not die and he erases her memories as a precaution. Even if she dies, he doesn't give a damn about the girl.

He walks towards the manor where they all gather together frequently. The other four members of the gang are there, sitting around the huge oak table, doing some research. "Anything new?" he shoots. His tone as well as his posture convey his anger. This vampire is about to explode!

"We'd go faster if we knew what we were looking for exactly," Dark ventures, "We know nothing about those two females."

"The one with the long black hair is called Angel. She's an executive assistant. The other one is called Camilla. That's all I know."

"That's much more than what we know!"

"I need to let off steam."

"Bad night?" Slash asks.

"The word isn't strong enough!" Kral spits before swearing.

"Go work out or something, it usually helps you."

Slash is right. Sport has always helped him calm down. He heads for the exercise room without further ado. He throws his white coat on the bench by the entrance door and without even taking the time to get changed, starts hitting a punching bag repeatedly. He can't stop thinking about the way he yelled at her. How could he be so stupid? He could have erased her memories in the hope of seeing her again but it just wouldn't be fair. And anyway, since when does he care about fairness? That woman has a strange effect on him. Right, left, and right again. It doesn't help him relax. He is furious, completely beside himself.

"What's going on, boss?"

He keeps on punching even though he recognized Slash's voice. It's not like he can just tell him about the feelings he has for that girl! It would be like putting himself down and Kraler isn't that kind of man. He throws punches at the bag again and again. Slash keeps still, watching him fascinated. Finally, the vampire leader stops.

"I totally fucked up," he pants.

"How?"

"I traumatized this poor girl for no reason."

"Since when do you care about girls?"

"It's the brunette we saw tonight."

"Yeah, I know. You took her to your office the other night."

Kral remembers. She had managed to release all his tension just by putting her soft hands on his shoulders. What a wonderful memory. He pushes the thought away. She will never do it again. "She knows nothing about the soldiers and I figured it out too late. I was in a blind rage."

"Did you see her again?"

"I went to her place earlier."

"You know where she lives?"

"It doesn't matter. Don't you understand?" he barks, "She won't see me again because she knows I'm a vampire and because I accused of being in the military!" He regrets his words instantly. He said too much. Slash may be his best friend, the one he confides in when something serious happens, but he never talks to him about... about what, exactly?

"Uh yeah, yeah I understand perfectly. You're completely smitten over her," Slash concludes.

"Nonsense!" Kral snarls.

But his friend doesn't believe him and decides to give him some advise. "I would suggest you apologize to her."

"Done that."

"Well, erase her memories then! What the hell do you care?"

"I won't do that to her."

"Okay. The boss is in love!" he snorts.

"Shut the hell up, I'm being serious!" Kraler roars, overwhelmed by his lack of self-control. Plus, Slash is getting on his nerves too.

"I got that. That female found a way to break your shell."

"That's not what it's about!"

"Really?" Slash stares at him with a skeptical look on his face. He still doesn't believe him but he doesn't expect his leader to admit that he has feelings for the human girl anyway. "What is it about, then?"

No answer comes. Kral fails at finding another lie to cover up. He's already said too much to his curious friend. He should have just kept on hitting that stupid heavy bag. The poor thing has always been his best outlet for unwinding.

Faced with his leader's silence, Slash understands that he was spot on. He could tease him some more, but he can see how wound-up Kral already is. He's like a bomb about to explode. However, he knows how he could reason with him and help him calm down. "You should go and see her."

"She'll kill me," Kral objects.

Slash has to refrain from laughing. A human girl killing Kraler? That would never happen. Even a soldier couldn't kill the guy. Kraler is way too quick. "She's probably sleeping. Just go watch her sleep, it'll help you cool off."

Kral ponders over the idea for a moment. It would be wonderful to see her at peace and asleep. "I'm not in love with her!" he shouts before grabbing his coat and storming out of the room, leaving Slash to laugh by himself.

"Of course you are. You're just going to need time to accept it," he mumbles to himself. The conclusion seems obvious. He will keep to himself, though. Kral wouldn't forgive him if he ever told the others.

Kraler teleports himself into Angel's kitchen. He sometimes uses this power although he usually prefers to walk. Right now he just feels completely stressed out and urgently needs to cool down. He heads for her room but finds her bed empty. Could it be that she isn't sleeping yet? He doesn't want to argue with her. He would lose his temper if she raised her voice and he would draw the life out of her just to calm himself down. He spins on his heels, ready to leave – it is just too risky – when his eyes fall on Angel's figure, lying down on the couch. He takes a few steps forward and notes that she is asleep. He looks at her for a moment before cradling her between his arms and taking her upstairs to her room where he slowly releases her body on the mattress, takes her shoes off and tuck her in. She moves in her sleep while he sits down on the edge of the bed and gazes at her. Her eyes are swollen, she must have cried a lot.

I'm such an idiot!

A wave of guilt washes through him. He runs his hand in her hair before brushing her face with his fingers. Slash's words echo in his mind. *The boss is in love.* In love? How could he ever admit it? Him, infatuated with this human girl. She would be in danger with him. He must let it go and accept the fact that he won't see her again. She doesn't want to see him again anyway, so it should be easy. He will disappear from her life. They hadn't been going out together for a long time after all. Upon reflection, they hadn't been going out at all. He once showed up to give her pleasure, and that was it. He has to admit that he enjoyed making love to her, much more than to all these women who spread their legs every time he walks by them. It was so much different with her. But it's over. In one last caress, he slides his fingers across her mouth before pressing his lips onto hers. Then, he vanishes.

It is only after the fourth time her alarm clock rings that Angel decides to get up. Surprise rocks through her as she notices that she is in her bed. She doesn't remember how she got there. She remembers what happened when she got home and that she fell asleep on the couch after crying her eyes out. Not only did Kral scare her to death, he broke her heart without realizing it. Unwilling to think about the vampire, she wards off that thought and starts getting ready for her last day of work before the weekend. Angel hasn't seen Amanda and Sally since Monday and she is quite happy about it. However, she comes across them on her way to the coffee machine.

"Hi Angel," they both say at the same time.

She replies politely while sliding a coin into the machine slot, then selects "double espresso".

"So? Do you believe that Byzance is a vampires' lair now?"

"Yes."

"Great!"

Amanda smirks but doesn't say anything. Angel grabs her coffee and starts making a move but she holds her back. "The guy who owns the place is an amazing lover."

Angel glares at her, shocked. Why does she feel the need to tell her such a thing?

"Sally and I spent some time at the bar... and in his arms."

Both of them slept with Kraler? Angel thought they were nice girls... maybe she misjudged them after all, maybe their colleagues were right about them from the very beginning. The bitches!

"He's an amazing fuck, but he doesn't kiss," Amanda continues, too happy to talk about her love affair.

Angel mulls over this new revelation.

"It's too intimate for him," Sally adds.

"And why are you telling me this, exactly?" The girls exchange looks, waiting for the other to reply but Angel answers her own question, "To show off, obviously. Just so you know, I've slept with Kral too. Twice. He's a good fuck, yeah. Oh and... he kissed me," she says before storming off. Who the hell do they think they are? They didn't pick the right morning to mess with her!

CHAPTER 10

That very night, Camilla pays a visit to Angel. She would like to hear her opinion about the previous night, and especially about David. She hopes her friend likes him and his pals. She can picture her with Kevin and she knows he might be interested. David told her. Nobody can resist Angel! Not only is she beautiful and charming, but she has a mysterious air about her that men are fond of. Camilla wants to comfort her sister. She rings the doorbell and an exhausted-looking Angel opens the door.

"Looks like someone didn't get much sleep last night!"

"Do you remember how late it was when we left the club? And Kraler was waiting for me here."

"Kral, really?"

Camilla asks Angel about the broken table as soon as she steps into the kitchen. What the hell happened, a hurricane? More like a striking lightning bolt!

"I told you, Kral came by."

"He did this?"

"He was beside himself."

"Because you stood him up?"

"Yeah right," she hisses, then walks into the living room, followed by Camilla. "He accused me of being part of some sort of vampire-killer gang. I don't remember the word he used to describe them. I was terrified," she tells, sitting down on the couch.

"I can imagine. But why did he accuse you of such a thing?"

"Not a clue." Still under the shock, Angel forgets that he also accused the boys they were with last night. The only thing she can remember is the way he yelled at her.

"Thank god he unleashed his anger on the table."

"I never want to see that bastard again."

"Alright. And apart from that, did you enjoy yourself last night?"

"Yeah, it was fun."

"How about David?"

"He seems very nice. And very much into you," she smirks.

That comment brings a smile to Camilla's face who can feel herself falling for the boy. "How about Kevin?"

"A bit annoying. Don't you think?"

"Oh Angel, make an effort! He likes you."

"Not mutual, sorry."

"I know you usually go for dark handsome guys but the one you picked is a total douche! He's a looney, if you want to know what I think."

"I know." She swallows hard, memories from the previous night rushing back into her mind. Even if she was exhausted, frightened and even if she forgot half of what happened, she really thought she was going to die.

"You deserve so much better."

"I won't see him again, don't worry."

"Do you feel like going out again tomorrow evening? We could go see a movie and then spend the night at *Retro*."

"I'm not sure, I'm really tired."

"Let's talk about it again tomorrow, okay?" Camilla insists, very intent on taking her friend out of the house.

"If you want."

"I'm meeting David later."

Angel lifts up an eyebrow and smiles as she notes how her friend's face glows every time she pronounces the name of her boyfriend. Camilla kisses her gently on the cheek before leaving so she can get some sleep. Angel is just about to die of exhaustion but try as she might, she cannot seem to fall asleep. It is still early but given how tired she was, it should have been a piece of cake. She tosses and turns in her big bed. Her undisciplined mind keeps drifting to Kraler. She would like to stop thinking about him, but it seems impossible. He obsesses her. The memory of him is imprinted in her cells and she misses him. It is a horrible sensation. She misses a vampire... and a very bad-tempered one too! She wants him out of her head, but there is nothing she can do. Plus, what Sally and Amanda told her doesn't help at all.

He doesn't kiss. It's too intimate.

It is quite disturbing as most people consider sex to be more intimate than a simple kiss. At least she thinks so, but apparently not Kraler. He kissed *her*. What is that supposed to mean? That he cares about her? If only. She would give anything to make it true. Then she scolds herself for having such thoughts. She had decided not to think about him anymore! She made the choice not to see him again. She must keep her distance. The guy is a vampire AND a lunatic! The kind of man she should be running away from.

She finally falls asleep, but her night is fitful and her dreams filled with images of Kraler.

Tonight, David has planned a romantic dinner with Camilla. She likes being alone with him so she couldn't be happier. After the delicious meal, they sit down in the living room with a glass of champagne. David didn't do things by half.

"I'm worried about Angel," she confesses.

"Why? She seems to be doing fine."

"That's what she keeps saying, but I'm sure she's only pretending."

"It's just a little heartache."

She has told David about Angel's problems with men before but without giving him too many details about her private life. "Yeah, I guess." She takes the glass to her lips and takes a few sips.

"I wish I were one of these bubbles. I would caress your tongue as drink me," David coos.

"I have better to suggest."

"Tell me."

She puts her glass down before sealing his lips into a passionate kiss. Their tongues touch timidly then caress one another softly.

"Yep, that's much better."

She picks up her glass and drinks the rest of her wine. David gives her a refill. "If I didn't know you, I'd think you were trying to get me drunk."

He grins. What a smile he has! She finds him sexy and beautiful. He is quite ordinary though: short brown hair, beautiful blue eyes and a stubble.

"I'll get what I want anyway," he says, waggling his eyebrows.

"You sure will," she answers, biting her lip. Her boyfriend has a strong sex drive and she likes it. She downs her second glass, feeling tipsy already. Camilla can't hold her drink. Some fall asleep, others go wild or get sick, but she tends to become very chatty. "Maybe we can move on to the next level."

"No time to lose," he replies, propping himself up from the couch. His phone starts ringing as he starts walking towards the bedroom. He excuses himself – he can't let it ring, it might be important – and picks up as the screen reads *Kevin*. "Something wrong?"

"*No*," his friend replies reassuring him, "*I just wanted to know if we're still going out tomorrow night. Is Angel coming too?*"

"Uhm, wait a sec," he says, casting a look at Camilla before asking her the question.

"I asked her but she said she wasn't sure. I'll talk to her tomorrow."

David recounts her answer to his colleague.

"Ok, got it. Let me know."

"No problem," David hangs up the phone. He hates being disturbed for stupid things while he's doing something important. Or when he is in charming company. "She's not feeling it, is she? She didn't have fun, last night?"

"She did, but she was tired and... you know what? He broke her kitchen table."

"Who did?"

"The guy she went out with for a short while."

"How did he do that? And why? Because of yesterday?"

"No. She told me he yelled at her. He was waiting for her when she got home."

"What the hell? Did she come home too late to his liking?" he asks, pulling her into the room.

"He accuses her of being part of a vampire-killer gang," she laughs.

David freezes. "What are you talking about? Why would he say that?" he tries to hide his turmoil because she doesn't know who he really is, and he intends to keep it that way.

"I don't know."

"Who is that guy your friend's been seeing?"

"A vampire."

"Ok," he sighs. He didn't want to hear that word. He doesn't want to have to do something against him, especially if he knows who and his friends are.

"His name is Kraler. Apparently he owns *Byzance*. You know, the club in south Seattle?"

Oh yes, he does know! He runs his hand over his face. Camilla's best friend is going out with the vampire he's supposed to be killing! Fucking nightmare. Moreover, he just realized the guy knows who he is. He can't just stay here and have fun with his girlfriend now. He needs to see the guys and tell them the fucking news!

"Camilla, I'm going to have to leave you for a moment." There is uneasiness in his voice. Not only because he's about to leave her there but also because he doesn't like the sound of it all. It can't end well. And why is Angel fooling around with a vampire? Couldn't she find someone else? How is he supposed to react? He must find out what to do.

"Why?"

"I'm sorry, babe. I'll try and be quick," he says softly, brushing his fingers across her cheeks.

"It's because of Angel and the vampire?"

"Only because of the vampire. I would prefer if you didn't ask any more questions."

"And I would prefer if you told me what's going on."

He hesitates. Can he confide in her? Does he even have a choice? If he doesn't tell her anything, he will lose her. "I will when I get back, I promise." He kisses her on the lips before heading off. That's another thing he's going to have to tell the guys about: Camilla has questions.

As soon as David is in the street, he calls Kevin, Bastien and Alan. He needs to meet them at *Retro*, the only place they consider as their headquarters.

CHAPTER 11

David casts a sullen look at his fellow soldiers before telling them that Angel is in involved with a vampire. Their eyes widen and they exchange surprised looks.

"What kind of vampire?" Kevin asks as his hopes of going out with the young girl shatter all at once.

"According to Camilla, it's the owner of *Byzance*."

"No less! The monster himself," Alan snarls.

"What do you mean they're *involved*?"

"I guess she must have slept with him. He was waiting for her on her porch last night and broke her kitchen table, accusing her to be one of us. He must have seen her hanging out with us."

"So he knows who we are!" Kevin exclaims, stunned, "That's the last thing we needed."

"What shall we do? Kill them as quickly as possible?" Bastien suggests.

"We're paid to eliminate the Snakes," David replies.

"And that's exactly what we're going to do... tonight," Kevin adds.

They all want to believe it, but they know it won't be easy. They were given this mission a while ago and understood very quickly that it would be a tricky and very risky one. The Snakes had killed all the troops that had been sent after them and they won't stop. They know they must be very careful. Their only plan of action was to take them by surprise, but that isn't an option anymore now that the vampire gang knows what they look like.

"Yeah, but how?" David prompts.

"We need a plan," Alan declares.

"Let's think about it and meet here again tomorrow."

"Weren't we supposed to see the girls tomorrow night?" Kevin reminds them.

"By the way, Camilla's been asking me questions."

"What did you tell her?"

"That I'd talk to her when I get back but I obviously can't do that."

"Why not? You should tell Angel too, that way she'll keep away from that mangy dog."

David ponders over the idea and ends up finding a solution. It could even be *the* solution. The plan that would cause the downfall of the vampire. Angel would set up a trap for him. The boys discuss the idea after David speaks it out loud. They will try it out tomorrow night.

"Anything new about the girls?" Kraler asks after stepping into the huge dining room in the manor.

"Apparently, Camilla is the soldiers' leader's girlfriend," Viper announces.

"Interesting." Kraler isn't sure how yet but that will definitely be an advantage sooner or later.

"They're not related."

"I know that. What else?"

"Just some random crap about their jobs. They're not in the military and they don't know about their little friends' secret mission."

That only confirms what Kraler already knew: Angel didn't know anything. *I'm such an imbecile!* He hates the way he behaved with her. Why did he have to yell at her like he did? He should have stayed focused on what she had said. He should have comforted her and tell her about his race. He regrets his words so badly now.

"The soldiers spend most of their time at Retro, I suggest we attack them when they make an exit tomorrow."

Kral glares at Dark. The idea might be good... or bad. Rushing in isn't always the best thing to do, especially now that they know about Camilla. "Do you have the address of that Camilla girl?"

Viper holds out a piece of paper with the address scribbled on it. Kral takes it, nodding. There's their solution! All they need to do is go a little deeper, and that's exactly what he's going to do now.

When David steps into his apartment, Camilla is asleep. He gazes at her for a moment without waking her even though they need to talk. He caresses her forehead and her eyes open. "David," she whispers.

"I didn't mean to wake you. Go back to sleep."

"We need to talk."

He sits down on the edge of the bed and pulls her against him. Camilla senses immediately that something is wrong. "What's going on?" she prompts, sitting up.

"I'm a soldier."

She stares at him in bewilderment. She already knows that.

"So are my friends." There is pain in his voice, as if the conversation is hurting him. "We have a very specific mission, which our predecessors failed to achieve. They have all been killed and we will be too if we don't succeed very quickly."

"What is the mission?"

"Exterminate the five members of a gang who call themselves the Snakes and who think they're the kings of south Seattle."

"Who are you talking about?"

"The vampires."

"Kraler," she understands right away.

"That bastard and his four buddies."

Camilla muffles a cry. She now understands why he was so reluctant to tell her what was happening. She had no idea such a mission could even exist.

"They've killed all the troops that the army sent after them so far."

"But you..." The words die in her throat. An awful feeling of fear prickles across her skin and she knows she is going to have to live with it from now on. What she doesn't know, is whether she will be capable of doing that.

"We won't let them kill us. We have a plan."

"A good one, I hope."

"We need to set up a trap for their leader."

"How?"

"We need your friend to help us. He won't be suspicious if she asks him to follow her."

"He thinks she's one of you guys. He'll never trust her."

"She'll have to make use of her power of persuasion."

"She'll never accept, and it's way too dangerous anyway."

"She won't risk anything, we'll be there to protect her. Let me talk to her about it."

"I won't stop you. You can tell her about your plan, but it's her call."

He nods in agreement before telling her that Angel needs to come to *Retro* the next evening so they can talk it through. It's a lot to take in for Camilla. David is a vampire killer who is after an unattainable gang leader. Moreover, he wants to use her heart-sister to accomplish that mission, which might cost him his life if he fails. If Angel refuses, she will lose the man she loves, but she can't ask her to accept to do such a thing. It would be dangerous and she isn't even sure the set-up would work.

Darkness has just fallen when the girls join David, Kevin, Bastien and Alan at *Retro*. Angel didn't really feel like coming but Camilla insisted that her presence was necessary. She naively imagines that her sister is trying to set her up with Kevin but she has no idea what awaits her.

David doesn't waste a minute. He sends Kevin off to buy them some drinks while he begins an explanation about their secret mission. She had heard it from Camilla but she shudders as he tells her exactly *what* the mission is about. Understanding, David gives her a moment to take it all in. As soon as Alan clinks their glasses down on their table, she gulps hers down in a few seconds. "It was vodka!" Alan informs her.

Angel keeps silent and puts her glass down before staring at David. "Why are you telling me all this?"

"I know you're more or less involved with the owner of *Byzance*."

"It's over," she claims.

"He's dangerous. I heard he smashed your table."

She lowers her gaze and confirms in a whisper. He had scared her to death that night and the memory is still vivid and painful.

"Would you accept to help us?"

"How?"

"By luring him out of his club, alone."

"So you can attack him then?"

"That's the idea."

She doesn't reply, incapable of imagining herself serving anybody up to be killed. But he isn't human... so maybe she would be better off shoving her qualms away and helping the soldiers around her.

"If we don't kill him and the others now, they'll end up killing us the way they killed our predecessors," David points out.

Camilla snuggles up against him. The idea terrifies her. Angel notes the spark of fear at the bottom of her sister's eyes. The fear of losing the one she loves. It breaks her heart. She would never let such a thing happen. She can prevent her from suffering, so why not do what it takes? "When?"

"An hour from now."

"Where?"

"You should think about it carefully Angel, it might be a two-edged situation," Camilla intervenes, worried.

"I know." She witnessed his strength and his rage, and the last thing she wants is to witness it again. Plus, she doesn't want that guy in her life. And if she had to choose between his life and David's, she would choose David's without a moment's hesitation. "Where?" she asks him again.

He tells her about the details of the plan and an hour later, Angel strides out of *Retro*.

As her steps take her to Byzance, Angeline doesn't let herself question her decision. She absolutely mustn't think about whether it is wrong or right, good or bad. She is doing it for Camilla. She saw the fear in her eyes. David is a good man, he doesn't deserve to die like this. Despite her reluctance to ponder over her choice, her mind keeps focusing on what she is about to do. Set up a trap for Kraler. Let's hope he doesn't realize what's going on... it would be so easy for him to kill her if he did.

The streets are crowded despite the overbearing darkness but the closer she gets to the south district, the more people seem strange. She had never noticed it before, but now the fear in their eyes as they glance at passers-by around them. A lot of people are gazing at a beautiful woman walking casually towards a restaurant. A female vampire. It is as if Angel had gotten rid of her blinders. She is now able to distinguish the human species from the vampire one in one single glance. How strange.

As she crosses the invisible line separating the city center from the south district an eerie sensation tickles at her scalp. It isn't fear – although it should be – but apprehension. Now that she knows what is happening here, she doesn't see the area in the same light, even though it isn't the first time she walks this path. She knows those sidewalks, those wooden benches scattered here and there, those trees dancing in the wind. But everything seems different tonight. The neighborhood is in the hands of vampires and they're far from being altar boys and girls, from what David told her. He explained that there were two types of blood-drinkers: the good ones, and the bad ones. Same goes in every species. The soldiers aren't looking to hurt the good ones, although they must keep an eye on them too, but they must exterminate the bad ones. He told her they refuse to drink blood from animals or synthetic blood. They only feed from humans and either kill them or erase their memories afterwards. She imagines Kral drinking blood.

How gruesome!

Plus, she could have been his victim. How stupid of her to fool around with a guy like this. She had no idea though... But how could she not figure it out when she can now spot them in a matter of seconds? This will remain a mystery. She doesn't really want to understand it though. Ever. After tonight, all this will be over.

CHAPTER 12

Byzance is full of people tonight, just like every Friday. As soon as she steps in, Angel notices that most of the customers here are vampires. The feeling is a bit unsettling, but she tries to stay focused; she is on a mission. She starts for the counter, where Stefan is bustling about. He's a vampire. She could have sworn he was human the first time she saw him.

"Hey Angel," he smiles at her. He is incredibly attractive. Is that a common trait amongst them? "What would you like?"

"I'm looking for Kral."

"He isn't here yet."

Apparently not. With a sigh, she sits down on one of the high stools. "A vodka." She is conscious of the fact that it might be better to keep a clear mind but unlike Camilla, she doesn't lose her connection with reality after one or two drinks. A bit of alcohol might boost her courage... and God knows she's going to need it. She pays for her drink before gulping down her drink.

"You waiting for someone?"

"No, I just want to talk to Kral."

"He shouldn't be long," he replies before serving another customer.

He had better not be! She doesn't want to spend her evening sitting on a stool waiting for him. She might start questioning her decision again and it would be a very dangerous thing. She is on a mission, and she will stick to the plan.

"Want anything else? It's on the house."

"I'd rather keep my mind clear."

"A soda, maybe?"

"Coke." Best to go for something soft. He puts the drink down in front of her and she takes a sip. The Coke is ice cold, which is very pleasant given the steamy atmosphere in the club.

"Hey Stefan! Can you get me five whiskies?"

Angel turns her head mechanically to look at the man. No, the vampire. It's Friz.

"Hi Friz," the bartender replies, handing him his drinks.

Friz takes them and strides off and towards a table where Kral and the rest of the gang are seated. Vampires too. David calls them the Snakes. Why? She doesn't quite know. She pulls her phone out and sends a text to Camilla.

He's here.

Putting the cell back in her purse, she suddenly feels a warm hand on her shoulder. She turns around to face Kraler.

"What are you doing here?" There is no agressiveness in his voice, just sheer surprise. He is definitely a vampire. Very odd, that new ability to recognize them.

"I need to talk to you."

He motions for her to follow him. She abandons her half-full glass of Coke and trails behind this divinely beautiful creature as he takes her into his office. She isn't happy about it; she needs to lure him out of the club and towards the appointed location.

"I'm listening." Kraler slumps down in his big armchair, looking casual although he is far from feeling relaxed. He wonders whether her presence here is a good or a bad thing. He will find out soon enough, surely.

"Not here."

"Where do you want to go?"

"We could walk."

He flashes a smile. As if he were going to walk with her in the street when it's so dark outside! He could do it – the darkness doesn't bother him, as opposed to sunlight – but what happened recently still tugs at his mind. He thought she was a vampire killer and even if she isn't, she is friends with the soldiers. So the truth is, he still doesn't trust her. "Why?" Yet again, he wants to trust her. He would like for her to forgive him. He has completely changed since that night. He is constantly irritated and even if he tries to hide it, he feels that he could explode at any moment.

"This is a vampire lair, if I'm not mistaken."

"True."

"I don't feel comfortable here."

"Nothing will happen to you."

"You don't want to," she observes sadly, "I never should have come here." She moves swiftly across the room and towards the door, but Kral comes blocking the way.

"Don't go. I'm glad you came."

"Really?"

He must fight his instinct to refrain from touching her face. He longs to caress her, his whole body is burning and demanding that he yields to the urge.

He can hear Angel's heartbeat; she is disconcerted... or scared. *Please tell me she isn't scared of me.* "Angel," he breathes, lifting his hand up to cup her face. He cannot fight any longer, his muscles are turning into marshmallow. With his thumb, he smoothes the young woman's cheek, immense pleasure surging through him. His finger traces the shape of her mouth. "I thought I'd never see you again." His jeans are becoming way too tight to hold his erection. "We'll go anyhere you want," he finally agrees.

Angel's heart is going completely wild. She doesn't control anything anymore, not even her reactions. She wanted to be strong, but she feels herself melting as Kral kisses her. He wraps his arms around her waist and she wraps her around his neck. He lifts her up and pins her against the door, kissing her feverishly. She had forgotten how good it felt to feel him against her body. She doesn't feel scared or threatened. The only thing she can feel coming off him is the desire pulsating through his veins. She desires him just as much, especially now that she can feel his lower stomach pressed against her.

"Kral," she murmurs between two kisses, "Stop it, please."

"Excuse me." He seems really sorry and unable to control his own body. He releases his embrace, putting her back down on the floor before walking back to his desk, swearing. What was he hoping for? He hates that he didn't manage to control himself.

"We need to talk." She tries to sound firm but he baffles her and it is becoming more and more difficult to stay calm. He spins on his heels to face her, leaning against the desk and crossing his arms and legs. "But not here." She forces a thought into her head: he's just vampire. A monster that must be killed before it harms anyone else. Nothing more. Kral heads for the door but as his hand grasps the handle, she cries, "No!"

"What?"

She feels torn. He isn't a monster but the man she desperately loves. Yes, she loves him. She could never accept to live without him. She couldn't. She would just die off. Everything seems so clear to her now. She's in love. Irrevocably in love. "I love you..." The words just slipped out of her mouth, but she doesn't regret them. She nervously waits for his reaction.

"Angel," he murmurs, taking a step towards her, "I wish you would forgive me."

Why? Because he doesn't love her, of course, and he is sorry that she fell stupidly in love with him. She must seem so pathetic to him. She feels like a complete idiot and would like to disappear from the surface of the Earth.

His hand brushes the top of her hair before running down her long black hair. "I didn't want to admit it, but you've awakened something very odd inside of me." He caresses her her throat and her left breast, and lingers on her slightly visible stomach.

"Knowing that you feel the same way is so... unexpected." He has feelings for her. She doesn't feel as stupid as before all of a sudden. She had told him *I love you* before, but apart from smiling widely, he hadn't said anything.

"I'm far from being perfect. I'm a vampire who doesn't give a shit about society and who kills for his own pleasure. I won't change. But if your love for me is strong enough, then I promise I won't disappoint you."

She hears the words but can't take them in. The only thing that matters to her in that moment is that he is willing to try and build something with her. She wraps her arms around his waist and pulls him against her. Their embrace lasts a long moment. The effect he has on her is so powerful she feels as if her heart and arteries are about to burst. He lays a kiss on top of her head and locks eyes with her. "I love you, Angel."

She can't breathe anymore. She almost chokes at his words and tightens her embrace around his body, finding it more and more difficult to calm down. She is close to tears. His fingers brush gently up and down her back, soothing her. She finally manages to breathe normally again and reluctantly loosens her grip, stepping back to kiss him.

They share a soft and sensual kiss before Kral asks, "So? Where did you want to go?"

"I don't want to go there anymore."

"Why?"

"It was a set-up," she admits shamefully.

He releases her and takes a few steps backwards. The sudden fear that this revelation might end their relationship forever strikes her.

"A set-up? What do you mean?"

"I'm sorry."

"Angel!" His tone is authoritarian. He wants to know what this is all about and he did the wrong thing opening up to that female human.

"Camilla and I don't know anything about it. They only told us who they are and the mission they need to accomplish recently."

"The soldiers?"

"They asked me to lure you outside of the club and into a dark street so they can attack you."

Her gaze drop. She can't look him in the eyes while she tells him about what she had agreed to do.

"Look at me," he demands. She timidly raises her head and briefly meets his stare. "You agreed to this?"

67

"I'm backing out."

"How am I supposed to believe you?"

"I'm begging you, Kral," she starts crying. Her eyes full of tears and her imploring won't change anything. He didn't know whether he could trust her or not but considering what she just told him, it is definitely going to be impossible. He sees it as a betrayal. However, it isn't the right time nor the right place to talk about it and there is another problem he must solve. "Where are they waiting?"

"Riverton Boulevard. They're waiting in the park by the patch with all the trees."

"I know the place."

"I was bitter when you left my house the other day. For my defense, I didn't know what to think."

"We'll talk about this later when we're just the two of us. Go home. I'll meet you there." Without adding anything, he storms out of his office.

"Kral?" she calls. Too late. The door slams shut behind him.

She hurries out of the room and follows him. He is leaving, flanked by his gang. They are going to the park. She knows it but there is nothing she can do to stop them. She makes her way out of *Byzance* but can't see them in the street, they've already disappeared. She calls Camilla who picks up right away. "Tell them to go home," she says, fear in her voice.

"What's going on?"

"Oh Camilla, I couldn't do it. I love him so much," she cries.

"Angel, tell me what's going on."

"Kraler and the other vampires. They're heading towards the park."

"Oh my god," Camilla sighs before hanging up.

Angel hopes that she will have the time to warn the soldiers. Or else... things might turn out very badly.

CHAPTER 13

The park is dark and full of trees. The perfect place for an ambush. Hiding in the darkness, the soldiers wait. They are armed and ready to exterminate the leader of the scumbag gang, that thing that recently killed a prostitute. The woman was found blood-drained and dead behind a garbage container. If it isn't one of Kraler's victims, it must be one of his peers'. It's all the same in the end. There are only five of them but they are all incredibly strong and agile. Those predators aren't easy to approach, let alone touch. So knowing that Kraler will be served to them on a silver platter nearly makes them reach ecstasy.

They are hiding behind some bushes, a few meters apart from one another so they can circle their victim. Their phones are off so that nothing can give them away. Lurking in the dark, they wait. Kraler arrives alone. David knows instantly that something is wrong. Unless Angel told him to wait for her there, which she might have done for her own safety.

"Go!" David shouts.

The soldiers jump out. Kral smiles, showing his sharp white fangs. He is surrounded by a bunch of soldiers, armed to the teeth, and he has a choice between the sword hooked into his belt or his gun. He opts for his sword because he likes to fight hand-to-hand. The soldiers are exulting, but David cannot help but notice the too-confident grin on the vampire's face. He understands what is going on when the four other Snakes appear out of nowhere, circling them. Now *they* are at the heart of the ambush.

What in the world happened? No time to ask questions. The battle begins between the two clans but the soldiers quickly come to understand that they need to back out now if they want to stay alive. It won't be easy, because the vampires don't go easy on them.

Angel begs Stefan to give her Kral's number. She needs to contact him as soon as possible so he ends up giving it to her, since the vampire's phone's SIMcard isn't traceable anyway. She hurriedly dials his number and calls him.

The battle continues with the vampires slowly gaining the advantage when a sudden vibrating sound brings everyone to a halt. Kraler's phone is ringing, and the soldiers run away as he picks up his phone, "Whoever the fuck you are, you're a dead man!"

Angel swallows. What a nice way to say *"Hello"*. Very bad timing, apparently. She feels even more guilty but she couldn't just let him murder her sister's boyfriend.

"I don't know your number, who the hell are you?"

If she doesn't say anything very quickly, he's going to grow even more irritated. *"It's me, Kral,"* she whispers.

"Angel?" His voice is calmer, which reassures her.

"Why the hell did you call me? You knew what I was going to do and I told you to wait at home. Are you home?"

"I'm standing in front of Byzance."

"Jesus Christ!" he hisses.

"Kral..."

"No! Go home. Now," he commands. "I'll be there soon," he adds in a slightly softer tone before hanging up.

"What's the matter?" Dark asks.

"The human girl is in heat?" Viper snorts.

Dark and the rest of them burst out laughing while Slash keeps silent, very much aware of his boss's feelings towards the girl. As a response, the vampire leader displays his sharp fangs. If he didn't have so much self-control, he would have pounced on these little bastards who find it funny. They think he is reacting that way because of his frustration. They have no idea that he is angry because of their teasing.

"Well, we won't get them tonight," Kral declares. "We can talk about stuff later at the manor. There's something I need to do first."

And he vanishes into the night.

Angel reaches her porch at the same time that Kraler materializes on her doorstep. She jumps back, not ready to talk with him and startled by the fact that he can teleport himself.

"Let's go inside," he says. His tone is domineering, but he doesn't sound angry. Angel relaxes a bit. Seems like the conversation won't be as heated as she had thought. She unlocks the door and moves to the side so her guest can come in. The broken table comes into display and a rush of guilt spreads through the vampire. "You haven't replaced it yet?"

"I haven't had the time. I need to go to the store, have it delivered and then set it up."

"I can take care of it."

"Look, you didn't come to talk about my table so let's get this over with."

They go into the living room and stand face to face in the middle of the room. "I don't know where to begin," he admits. Kral looks so genuinely confused that she decides to help him out by bringing up the subjects they need to discuss, one after the other.

"I couldn't just let you kill them."

He understands that she is referring to the soldiers. "Why not?"

"David is Camilla's boyfriend."

"I know but honestly, it doesn't change anything. You have to pick a side. It's either us or them," he barks. "And I don't intend to die any time soon!" He starts pacing across the small living room. Seriously, why is this room so small? He hates it here!

"There has to be another way."

"Yes there is." He turns around and fixes his stare into her beautiful green eyes. "The members of my community and myself would have to feed off synthetic blood exclusively and animal blood occasionally. We wouldn't be allowed to kill any more people and would have to follow human rules."

"Okay. So what's the problem?"

A spark of skepticism flares in his eyes. Is she really that stupid? Doesn't she know who she is? He will never submit, he is a rebel at heart. "I refuse it. We all refuse it. We'd rather keep on living the way we do and deal with the soldiers in our way."

"Why?"

"Only human blood allows us to keep our strength to its maximum."

Angel understands that the battle between soldiers and vampires is inevitable. All she did was postpone it. As to which clan would win the fight, there is no way of telling in advance. She could lose him.

"I'm sorry I disturbed you, but I'll do it again if I had to."

A grin flashes across his face. He didn't expect any less coming from her. "Why's that? Your life will end up being at stake."

"I want to be an ambassador of peace for you guys."

71

He lets out a snort. It is the first time she sees him laugh and it suits him perfectly. He should relax and let his hair down more often.

"Let me try."

"If you feel like it... I won't stop you."

It is her turn to smile as she takes a step closer to him. "I don't care what you are. I love you and I want you. Now and forever." When she first found out about his true nature, she got scared and wanted to run away from him, thinking that she might manage to forget him if she locked up her heart. What an incredible mistake she made by accepting to set him up tonight. She knows she loves him and the part of her who wouldn't stop pushing her in his arms is now content, as if that was where she belonged. As if it was her destiny. Kraler strokes his hands across her cheeks before running them down her long hair.

"I shall give you whatever you want but you must never betray me or try and trick me again."

"I tried to persuade myself that it would be the best thing to do for everyone..." she trails off. She regrets it so much, she never could have survived without him. He attracts her, and there is nothing she can do to fight that attraction. She has no resistance force. "We were meant to meet each other."

Nodding, he gazes at her tenderly. He thinks so too, even if he still cannot explain it. She is the first woman who managed to break his shell and who is still here despite the horrible things he's done and that he will do again. She may stupidly believe that she can save him and he lets her bask in her illusions even though he knows that her efforts are vain. He can feel her heartbeat quickening as he takes her hands out of her hair and places one on her chest and the other on her neck. Her chin strap. He perceives the blood pulsating within her veins and he closes his eyes to fully enjoy the whirring. His lips drew slightly over his fangs. He is willing to give her anything he has now that he has admitted his feelings for her and therefore, he also wants everything she can give him.

Seeing his sharp teeth, she shudders. The vision forces her to return to the earth. She is facing a vampire and he has one hand on her heart – the very organ of life – and another hand over her throat where he could easily drain her blood out if he decided to. "Kral?"

"Let me taste you," he demands, his eyes still closed. The source of his desire lies deep within his soul. He wants her so badly that if she said no, he would be capable of shattering everything he came across.

She swallows in response. She can't just let him do that. She doesn't know anything about the process and the risks it comprises. She definitely does not want to die tonight. "Kral, please."

He senses the fear in her voice. He can also feel her shaking a little. He realizes that went too far so he closes his mouth and his black eyes pop open. "I shouldn't have..." Seeming troubled, he takes her hands off her. He cannot stay here now that she said no, he must run away as fast as possible so he can explode without her seeing him, without running the risk to hurt her.

"Kral, look at me." She takes her hands in his, begging him to look at her. He complies. She is wonderfully desirable and her spicy floral fragrance tickles his throat. He is thirsty for her. He wants to drink her so badly and staying here only makes the urge more compelling.

"I'll give you everything you want but not this, not now... I don't know how... It scares me," she stammers. She can't find the right words to express herself properly. She can see that he is about to burst, she can see it in his eyes. "I want you to make love to me," she says, putting the vampire's hands down on her hips. She moves closer to him until she is pressed against his powerful body. Her smell is all over the place now but his anatomy doesn't react. He cannot have an erection although she is driving him insane. The only thing he is obsessed with right now is her blood, and if she keeps on shying away from him, he is afraid that he won't be able to hold back. His predatory instincts take over whatever little reason he has left. He breathes in the delicious and intoxicating smell before brushing his fangs against her soft skin.

CHAPTER 14

The doorbell rings suddenly, bringing Kraler back to reality. He releases his prey hurriedly and stares out at her confusingly, not realizing that he really was about to drink her blood. Disgusted by his beastly behavior, he winces at the two small marks his fangs have left on her throat. Her eyes are full of terror and she stands motionless, paralyzed by fear. The doorbell rings again and Kral teleports himself out.

Angel can neither move nor breathe, let alone think. Something terrible happened... something that cannot be described. He was about to drink her blood against her will. She trusted him blindly. She cannot seem to pull herself together; her limbs seem disconnected from her brain, her blood and organs are lacking in oxygen but she can't snap out of it and stumbles down.

"Angel!" Camilla calls, pounding on the door.

"Maybe she's not home," David puts in.

"Probably hanging out with the scumbag," Kevin hisses.

They are all standing in front of the door, waiting for their friend to let them in but nothing happens.

"Let's come back later," Camilla decides.

Kraler is angry at himself and cannot seem to cool off. He storms into the manor, frightening his peers who are usually quite used to his grumpiness. He has never been *this* angry, though. He heads directly for the exercise room where he throws his coat on the bench and starts unleashing his anger on the punching bag. It doesn't help. He can feel that something is wrong. Angel is in pain. It's his fault for sure. If he hadn't acted like a blood-thirsty predator, none of this would have happened. He realizes promptly that it isn't that kind of pain but something else. She is in danger. "Slash, come over here!"

The scar-faced man hurries into the room.

"Something weird is going on!"

"What?"

"I sense danger. She's dying." The next moment, he hits the wall hard with his fist, blaming himself all the more for hurting her.

"Your human girl?"

"Fuck! I would've drained all the blood out of her if it wasn't for that doorbell!" he shouts, angry at himself.

"You bit her?"

"I didn't have the time, thank God."

"So what are you on about?"

"She lives in Orcas St, number 12. Teleport yourself there immediately."

"Kral, I'm not sure she'll appreciate to see me suddenly appear in her living room."

"Do what you're told!"

The leader of the pack is about to burst. Slash accepts the order and dematerializes himself in front of him.

"Call her," David suggests.

Camilla complies and tries calling her friend. The phone starts ringing – they can hear it from where they are – which means that she is definitely home. "She must feel bad. Maybe she's afraid to open the door," Camilla winces.

"Angel, open that door! We just want to talk," David demands.

Slash materializes in the human girl's living room. Confusion washes over him until he notices a prone figure on the floor. It's her. He moves closer, bends down and checks her pulse. She isn't breathing anymore. Shit! Kral will kill him if he tells him the horrible news. He performs mouth-to-mouth resuscitation and then heart massage on the young woman. The next moment, she straightens up briskly, taking a deep, sudden inspiration. She can feel her organs burning and aching. She remembers Kral's fangs on her throat and turns her head to face a man she has never seen before. No, a vampire. Actually, she *has* seen him before.

"I'm Slash. You okay?"

She scrutinizes him; he has never been this close. His hair is very long and black. He has a horrible facial scar and black eyes like Kral. Even though he is squatting on his haunches, she can see that he is heavyset. And his intentions are good, from what she can tell.

"Do you want some water?"

She shakes her head. She needs to realize what happened, to understand, but the door swings open suddenly. The next moment, Camilla and the vampire-killers make their way into the living room.

"Back off!" David orders, pulling out his gun.

"Easy," Slash replies.

"I'm gonna end you, vampire!"

Slash rapidly assesses the situation; there are four of them and he is alone. They have guns, he doesn't. Whatever. He will fight against them if he needs to. He has recognized the (his) goddamn soldiers and the urge to beat the hell out of them is tempting but it isn't the right place for that. He is here for the pretty human still sitting on the floor. "You sure you're okay?" he asks Angel, ignoring the killers' threat.

She touches her throat with the tip of her fingers and feels something, probably the marks left by Kraler's teeth. She shudders.

"Did he touch you?" David asks her.

Her hand drops and he notices two small marks on her skin. He deduces in a flash that the ugly scar-faced man must have bitten her. If they hadn't barged in, he would have drawn her blood out. Aiming at the vampire, he shots.

"Scumbag!" Slash snarls, materializing directly into the exercise room.

Kraler stares at him. He is about to burst, his anger has reached its peak. "She's alright, don't worry, but the soldiers barged into her house and their stupid leader opened fire. I had no other choice but to..."

"They're in her house?" Kral interrupts him.

"Yes."

Promptly, the bad-tempered vampire dematerializes himself under Slash's eyes.

David is shocked to see that his target has disappeared. He hopes that he – at least – touched him, but nothing is less certain. Camilla hurries towards Angel as Kraler appears in the living room. Dressed in black, the warrior's face is dark and threatening. The young woman swallows hard, trying to pull her friend towards her but the vampire interposes himself, stepping in between the two girls and forcing Camilla to step backwards. Angel witnesses the scenes from a distance. She is not really present. She is in a lethargic state and nothing seems to make sense. She is still under the shock of what just happened. Kraler growls at the soldiers before squatting down near the young woman. He feels her pulse and observes that she is okay. He strokes his hand across her face and pulls her against him.

David watches the scene, fascinated. The vampire is in love! That's a scoop! He would have burst out laughing if it wasn't for Scarface who just materialized behind his leader. He aims his gun at him. He could kill her. Actually, that's exactly what he is going to do. Apparently, he didn't reach him the first time but he intends to hit bull's eye this time. All at once, another vampire appears, and then another, and another. The Snakes are all here. Fighting them in front of the girls and in the minority against the blood-thirsty monsters isn't the greatest of ideas if they want to stay alive. David lowers his gun and gestures to the others. It's time to get the hell out of here.

The vampires don't budge an inch. Second time they win the battle against those pathetic vampire killers without having to do much. Kraler carries Angel in his arms before straighting up and leaving the house with his gang.

CHAPTER 15

The soldiers walk for a few seconds before reaching what looks like a park. David sits down on a bench, feeling pathetic. Camilla must think he is ridiculous. "I can't stand that cold-blooded race!"

"You did the right thing. We couldn't attack them like this," Kavin affirms.

"Doesn't change a damn thing!"

"I don't care about your battle! All I can think of is the fact that Angel is with them!" Camilla yells.

"They won't hurt her."

"You don't know that!"

"Their stupid leader fell for her."

Kraler, in love with Angel? Camilla doesn't know whether she can actually believe that. She noticed the way he acted with her and she knows that he would have attacked them if they had moved closer but going so far as to say that he *loves* her...

"Believe me, she'll be fine," David reassures her, his gaze falling on her.

She would like to be as confident as he sounds but cannot. She can't pull herself together, let alone reason calmly. She is worried about her sister. "I saw the marks on her throat!" she hisses.

"So did I. Don't know how she got them."

"You guys are soldiers! You were supposed to protect her! You're just a bunch of losers!" Upon these words, she spins around and strides off towards the house of the only person she can't take her mind off. The cowards may not want to save her from those vampires, but she will.

David doesn't have the energy to go running after her. She is right and he feels even more lousy now that she has told him.

"We would have lost. They would have killed us," Alan declares.

"She's unfair," Bastien adds.

"No, she's right," Kevin admits. "We reacted like losers. We're duffers."

"They weren't here to fight but to protect their leader," David says. "If I had opened fire, they would have butchered us. And Camilla too."

78

They all know it. So does Kevin, even though he feels like a coward. What they did is intolerable. They're soldiers for God's sake! They should have done something. They might be dead by now but they might have killed at least one of them. Well... in the best case scenario.

Camilla ventures into Angel's house. She doesn't know if the vampires are still here, but she imagines that they must be. Kraler is probably here, for sure. "I'm Camilla, Angel's friend. I'm alone and I don't have a gun."

She quickly realizes that the living room is empty and she guesses that he must have taken her upstairs to her room. She doesn't know what happened, but she saw her friend's blank stare. It was serious. And if the scar-faced vampire had hurt her, Kral would have killed him. So what in the world had happened to Angel? She pushes the bedroom door open. Empty. She tries the other rooms to no avail. Angel isn't here anymore. They took her somewhere, but where?

"Angel?" she calls.

It is past 2AM. Kraler has been pacing for so long he has no idea exactly how long. Angel is being seen by a doctor of their race and he waits anxiously.

"She'll be fine," Slash assures him, joining him in the hall. The beige rug is starting to wear away. "Jesus Christ! Look at that rug... you killed it!"

Kraler shoots him a deadly glance. "I don't give a shit about the rug!"

"What did you do to her?"

He doesn't want to think about it. He runs a nervous hand over his face. What an idiot he is sometimes! "I... I wanted her, but I also wanted her blood and I started touching her heart and throat. Fuck... she smelled so good!"

Slash listens, perceiving the pain in his words. It mustn't be easy for such a solitary warrior like him to admit that he has feelings for a human. Worse, Kraler admits his weaknesses and the incredible effort must burn him on the inside.

"I asked her if I could taste her blood. I wasn't prepared for her refusal, but she said no. I tried to resist but I lost control and if that stupid doorbell hadn't brought me back to earth, I would have drunk all of her blood."

"You could erase her memories."

"I could... but I won't."

"And that's all to your credit, but you can't force her to stay here either. When she regains consciousness she's not going to want to stay."

"What was that ticke of danger I could feel?"

"She had stopped breathing."

Kraler gazes at him with no expression on his face. Slash feels bad about telling him the truth but he makes it up by adding that he saved her life.

"How?"

"If I tell you, you're going to beat the hell out of me," he snickers.

"Mouth-to-mouth resuscitation, of course."

"Don't worry, I didn't put any tongue and neither did she." He laughs quietly, refraining from bursting in loud guffaws because he can see Kraler becoming red with fury.

"Very funny!" he snarls.

The doctor, Slater Lawson, makes his way out of his patient's room, ending the mockery.

"She had a heart attack but she is fine now. I gave her a tranquilizer so she calms down and gets a bit of rest. She'll stay asleep for at least 24 hours. She is physically fine but emotionally very disturbed. I would advise you to erase her memories, gentlemen."

"Thank you Doctor," Slash says. "I'll walk you back."

A heart attack! Dear God, how could he do that to her? He hates himself. He should have controlled his impulses! He almost killed her! *Damn idiot!*

Once the two vampires have walked off, Kraler enters the softly lit room. His eyes flick to Angel who is lying down in her bed. Sleeping. She looks peaceful but she certainly isn't. Yet... erasing her memories? He can't. It wouldn't be fair to her. He moves closer and sits down on the edge of the bed, brushing a strand of hair off her face so he can stroke his hand across her delicate features. He has affection for that female, he loves her intensely and he wants her. He isn't thinking about her blood now but only about his pathetic misdemeanor. He breathes in her smell, a mix of lily and rose, slightly pulling the cover over her so she doesn't get cold.

"Forgive me, my love." His fingers trace her lips. He had wanted to make love to her and they would both be lying naked in a bed at this hour if it wasn't for his stupid behavior. He could touch her beautiful body he doesn't know by heart just yet. The first time they had had intercourse was in the ladies' room at *Byzance*. What an idiot he had been that night! Already then, he had wanted her, he had felt the attraction. The second time had been in her bed. It was marvellous and he had taken her several times.

He takes her hand off her but his gaze continues to linger on her.

"So what did old Doctor Lawson say?" Friz wants to know as Slash enters the living room.

"She's fine."

"Now that the human girl is in the clear, can somebody explain what the hell is going on?" Viper prompts.

"Why did he ask us to go to her house?" Viper adds.

Slash is taken by surprise. He isn't the one who should answer all their questions. "Kral will tell you in his own time."

"She's friends with the killers, she tried to set Kral up, we just want to know what's happening, that's all!" Viper insists.

"You're right," Kraler's voice answers as he steps into the spacious living room. It is time for him to talk even if he isn't sure how the others are going to take the news. Most of them are pretty much lone wolves who like to screw around. "The doctor advised me to erase her most recent memories but I won't do it. Perhaps you're wondering what happened to her... well, I tried to drink her blood without her consent."

He tells them the rest of the story without giving too many details, just the events he considers are the most important ones. Nobody blames him. He could have killed her for all they care, but he must explain why *he* would have cared. "Angel will stay here for as long as she desires."

"In what honor?" Viper snaps.

"Because I said so."

Viper stares at him for a moment and the two men hold each other's gaze. Unblinking, Kraler gives him a threatening look but Viper glare is just as terrifying. The leader doesn't lower his gaze, boiling on the inside. Viper finally looks down.

"Do you have something against it, Viper?"

"No."

"I... I have some very profound feelings for that human woman and I want her to be my partner."

The guys exchange glances. Kraler wants to share his life with that girl? That's ridiculous! The very idea of Kraler infatuated with a female sounds grotesque.

"How about her?" Friz ventures.

"She felt the same way before I screwed up."

"Kral, that female will become your weak point," Dark warns him.

"She already is. The soldiers aren't that stupid and they know how attached to her Kral is," Slash nods.

"Which makes things even more dangerous for us," Dark puts in.

81

Viper remains silent. He doesn't want another confrontation with the boss.

"Not as long as she stays here," Kral assures them.

"But is that even what she wants? You said you didn't want to make her forget what happened," Friz retorts.

"I do not know."

"Don't put us in danger."

"Of course I won't."

"As long as it doesn't have any impact on us, we'll accept her," Viper finally says. "But if and when she becomes a threat for us, she will have to be eliminated."

Kraler glowers at him. Nobody will ever hurt Angel.

Completely despondent, Camilla calls David to tell him about Angel's disappearance. The young man tries to comfort her to no avail; Camilla refuses to speak to him, she still blames him responsible for what happened and she wants him to find her friend.

CHAPTER 16

The soldiers enter their superior's office feeling very nervous. David is supposed to explain how they let the vampires slip away twice.

"Hello, unit V." The wing commander sits down behind his desk as the soldiers salute him. David swallows. The lieutenant colonel tends to lose his temper very quickly when something doesn't go his way.

"I'm listening. Tell me about your report."

"There aren't enough of us to fight the Snakes," David enunciates.

The lieutenant colonel seems to mull over the thought. He has a habit of twisting his goatee when he thinks. "How many more men?"

"There might only be five vampires but they're incredibly strong and agile. I think we could defeat them if we were twice as many as them."

"Twice as many!" Again, he twists his goatee around his fingers.

David doesn't think he is exaggerating by asking him to send them more soldiers. The four of them can't do much against the vampires and they all know it. David particularly knows, since Camilla won't talk to him because of that very reason. If there had been more of them, none of this would have happened. Starting with that ambush in the park that turned against them. They could have fought instead of running away like a bunch of cowards.

"I'll see what I can do for you, Captain Braida."

"Our mission would be over by now if there had been more of us."

"I understand. I have heard your request. Now, report!"

It is the moment they all feared. David is their leader, he is the one who must speak and take on the sanctions that might ensue if the lieutenant colonel deems them necessary. He can't mention Angel. Admitting that they used a civilian in order to lure the vampire leader out of his lair would put them in a very bad light. On the other hand, he has to talk about her disappearance. That way, it'll put the Snakes in an even worse light. He tells his boss about the kidnapping.

"Why kidnap that human girl?"

"We don't know but we are doing our best to figure it out."

Talking about the vampire's feelings would be inappropriate. Plus, it is only an assumption he wants to believe in to convince himself that Angel is not in danger. Moreover, vampires – but mostly Kraler – are known to be cruel and soulless; nobody will believe such fantasies. David keeps relating the recent events that took place, the aborted battle in the isolated park although it seemed like the perfect place. If Angel had brought him along on his own, he wouldn't have survived, that's for sure. They had planned everything and were armed to their teeth, ready to destroy him. The thing is, he minimized Angel's feelings towards Kral. She loves him, it's irrevocable. And that love will unfortunately not cause the vampire's downfall but her own. He finishes his account of the events by mentionning his presence as the kidnapping took place. He is forced to tell the lieutenant that she is one of his acquaintances, that she is his girlfriend's friend, but that is all he says.

Of course, the lieutenant colonel believes that they kidnapped her *because* she is the friend of David's partner. He is on the wrong track, but David keeps silent.

"Do everything you can to find that girl!"

Exactly what David was going to do, with or without his permission; the problem is, nobody has any idea where the vampire gang might live. They went through the south district several times without any success. They are probably looking in the wrong place and should try somewhere else. But where?

"I will send more soldiers to back you up, Captain Braida."

"Thank you, lieutenant colonel."

David doesn't have the energy to discuss the report with the three others and goes home directly afterwards. He needs to relax so he can think about the best thing to do. The only way to find Angel is to figure out where the vampires live. But those cunning warriors usually know when they are being tracked, so they need to be discreet. The sound of knocking on his door startles him. He wanted to stay alone, not see the whole unit show up at his house! He feels like a loser but he is going to have to deal with it. Sighing, he rises to his feet and heads for the door. He was mistaken. It is not his peers who turned up but...

"Camilla!" Once the surprise has washed off, he lets her in. Her face is closed and judging from her current state of mind, he had better not bring up the sensitive subject or else he might feel even worse.

"Have you heard from Angel?" Her voice is calm. That's a good sign. But is it going to last once he tells her that he doesn't have any news?

"They accepted to send more men in my unit to help up. We'll find her."

"In other words, you have no idea where she is."

"No, but I'm very sorry that I don't."

"They took her with them, didn't they?"

"I guess they did."

"Why?"

"I don't know."

"Do you think Kraler wants to get his revenge because of the trap Angel set for him?"

"Everything is possible. At this point, there is no way of telling even though I think he's in love with her and will not do anything that might hurt her."

Although she managed to keep her cool in the beginning, Camilla cannot hold back her anger any longer,"You don't know that! Don't give me that bullshit just to clear your conscience!"

"My conscience is far from being clear!" he yells. "I didn't even do anything to protect a civilian from a bunch of blood-thirsty monsters!"

"What are you doing now? You're at home pitying yourself instead of looking for her!"

"I don't know where to look! We have no idea where they live!"

"You're not making much effort..."

"You're being unfair, Camilla!"

"I'll find her myself, but don't count on me to give you any details!"

"Camilla?" he calls after her as she heads for the door. "Please, stay."

She can't, she just resents him too much. She wants to keep away from him for a while, at least until they find Angel. The sound of the door slamming shut breaks David's heart. Their couple is going astray and he knows it will keep getting worse until Angel is back.

Camilla doesn't think she is being unfair to David as she blames him for everything that happened. Starting with the moment he asked Angel to set up a trap for Kraler, putting her in danger. It is still early but she hasn't got anything to do, so she decides to go to *Byzance*.

The club is pretty quiet at this hour. Feeling completely lost, she tries to put up a facade by sitting down casually at a table. She glances around but of course, no vampire in sight. It isn't very surprising though. Rumor has it that they disintegrate in the sunlight. They might show up later when it is darker outside. She is determined to approach Kraler and to demand – yes, demand – that he lets Angel go, but also that he gives her an explanation. The image of

85

the two small marks on her sister's throat haunt her. She wants to know what happened!

She drinks a vodka and then a whisky. Aware of the fact that she can't hold her drink, she orders a Coke. An Orangina. A Sprite. *Jesus Christ! It's 11PM and they still haven't turned up.*

Byzance is packed but the vampires are absent. She lets out a sigh. All that waiting for nothing! Feeling exhausted, she yawns and decides to go and have a look around the room before she leaves. Suddenly, she spots them. The vampires... but no Kraler. Not wasting any time, she makes her way towards their table.

"Is Kraler here?"

Their eyes instantly flick to her. They recognize her. "The soldier's girlfriend!" Viper remembers. "Your stupid boyfriend didn't tell you it might be dangerous for you to come across one of us?"

Dangerous? Well... Yes.

They're blood-thirsty and she's their enemy's girlfriend. She hadn't really thought about that actually. All that matters to her is Angel. "I just want a word with Kraler."

"You worried about your friend?" he sniggers.

"Boss is taking good care of her if you know what I mean," Dark laughs before high-fiving his friend.

The blond guy, Friz, seems to belong to the same category. The arrogant bastard bursts out laughing along with them. "And the bitch always asks for more!" he adds.

Camilla rolls her eyes. *What a bunch of idiots.* She never imagined that such tough warriors could be so stupid. They're just a group of retarded teenagers!

"Don't be stupid, guys," Slash intervenes, "Kral would kill you if he heard you speak like that."

"Precious Angel," Viper mocks, "She'll cause his downfall! Our own downfall!" he snarls, getting up suddenly. He takes a step and another, until he is standing face-to-face with Camilla. Terrified, she takes a step backwards. She swallows hard as he curls his lip and bares his teeth at her.

"I'm gonna take care of her," he tells the others, "I'm gonna show her what it's like to get boned by a real male," he roars and then laughs out loud.

"Leave her alone," Slash objects, also getting up. "She wants to talk to Kraler... we must grant her request before doing anything else to her."

Viper sighs.

"Follow me, young lady," Slash demands.

"Young lady," Viper snorts before slumping back down in his seat.

Slash leads the human girl into Kraler's office. Closing the door, he apologizes for the others' child-like behavior. "They're worried about your friend's power on our leader."

"What power?" she asks, glancing around.

The office is large and has little furniture. There is plenty of space and the atmosphere is cozy. Kraler did the furnishing; he hates feeling smothered. "I've seen you with Angel before, I imagine you know what is going on between the two of them."

"Yes. What I didn't expect was to see two small holes in her throat." The memory makes her shudder. Thinking that her friend could have been that bastard's dinner... No!

"Don't worry, Kraler didn't touch her. But... he's a vampire, and she reeks of fresh blood."

"Where is Angel?"

"With Kraler."

"I want to see her."

"She's still sedated. She was restless and our doctor preferred to give her a tranquilizer so she can get some rest. She had a heart attack."

"What?" Camilla breathes, putting her hand over her mouth. Her legs suddenly feel very weak. A geart attack! Slash pulls an armchair behind her as she collapses.

"She's doing fine," he affirms.

"I want to see Kraler."

"It would be pointless. He won't leave her bedside until she opens her eyes."

"When?"

"During the night, probably."

"He won't hurt her, right?"

"No. Kral is... He told us about his intentions towards your friend. He wants to wed her."

Camilla's eyes pop open. *Wed* her? Nothing seems to make sense anymore since Angel met that vampire. "Is it possible for your race?"

"Yes it is. We don't celebrate at church, but we have our own traditions."

"Angel is human!"

"That isn't an obstacle."

"What if she says no?"

"Kral will definitely have a hard time."

"Is he in love with her?"

"Absolutely," he says, then laughs. Camilla notices the dimples in his cheeks, which add to his charisma. Actually, under the cold, dark facade hides a very attractive man. "It's the first time it happens to him. I'm sure he must feel quite embarrassed. He tried to fight his feelings, he didn't want to admit them. After all, I'm glad that he did."

"And the others are okay with this?"

"As lons as it doesn't create any problems for them."

"What sort of problems?" Camilla is surprised at herself for not feeling scared of the scar-faced vampire. She actually enjoys talking to him. He is friendly and not threatening at all, despite his frightening looks.

"The soldiers are tracking us. They don't approve the way we live and want us dead, but you already know that. The female represents Kraler's weakest point."

"The soldiers wouldn't harm Angel."

"Your friends probably wouldn't. Unit V," he smiles. "But if they don't succeed, they'll send some other troops after us, and those might not be as sympathetic."

Camilla realizes that if her friend – her sister – accepts to officialize her relationship with Kral, she will become a target for unscrupulous military men. Kraler will protect her and so will the other vampires, unless she becomes a danger for them. Then, they will kill her. She swallows hard. "Thanks for talking to me."

"You're welcome, young human."

She scribbles her telephone number on a piece of paper she found on Kral's desk before giving it to Slash.

"You want me to call you?" he smiles.

"No, Kraler. When Angel wakes up, I want to see her. I suppose she's not his prisoner."

"I'll give it to him," he accepts, taking the paper.

She heads for the door but just as she is about to open it, Slash materializes right in front of it, preventing her from leaving.

"I can't let you go. The others would consider it as an unforgivable mistake." He doesn't look so friendly anymore; he is frightening. "Kraler won't be able to see you now and if I take you to the manor, Viper might try and take advantage of you. He likes it when women resist him."

She had noticed, and she is sure that he would have been capable of shamelessly raping her right there on their table in front of the crowd.

"I suggest you stay at my place, until we have a word with the boss."

"I want to go home."

"It's impossible, young human. You came to us without thinking, you must bear the consequences of your actions."

She drops her gaze. *What kind of trouble have I put myself into?*

"We're going to use the back door. My Chevrolet is parked in the street. I'll drive you to my place before telling the warriors about it."

What other options does she have? Fighting against him? It would be a losing battle. She doesn't have a choice. He opens the door and kindly asks her to go first. He then follows her and leads her out of the building, using the emergency exit. As they approach his grey Chevrolet, he quickens his pace and opens the passenger door for her. Inside the car, he blindfolds her with a black scarf so she doesn't see where they go. During the ride, she doesn't feel any animosity coming from the vampire. He calls his friends to let them know what he did and then dials Kraler's number.

After he has parked the car, they get out of the vehicle and he guides her. They walk, get into an elevator, and walk again. Finally, he unties the blindfold. She is in the middle of a spacious apartment. A dark landscape is visible through the picture glasses.

"I thought vampires feared sunlight."

"That's true." He pushes a button and steel blinds roll out, covering up all the glass panes in the apartment.

CHAPTER 17

"What's ya name?"

"Camilla."

"Very pretty. I'm Slash."

She takes in the nicely decorated apartment. Nobody could guess that a vampire lives here. There is nothing black. No coffin. She smiles at the thought.

"I'm starving! I'm gonna make myself a sandwich. Do you want anything?"

"You eat? I mean..."

"Yes. Vampires don't only drink blood, they eat food too. Well, born vampires do. C'mon."

She follows him into the kitchen. *Wow!*

It is well-lit and very well-equipped. Who would have thought Slash liked to cook? Definitely not her. He opens the double-door refrigerator as she sits down on one of the four stools around the table in the center of the room.

"I'm gonna have a sandwich because I'm sure Kral is going to call me. I reached his voicemail earlier in the car."

She hadn't realized that. She had thought he had managed to reach him directly.

"Do you want one?" He gathers ham, butter, pickles, tomatoes and cheese before taking some bread out of a cupboard.

"Okay." She isn't feeling very hungry but seeing him prepare all these ingredients is enough to rouse her appetite. She watches him as he skillfully makes a medium sized sandwich. He spreads some butter inside the bread before placing the ham, the pickles cut out in small pieces, the tomato cut out in round slices and a few pieces of cheese. He then hands it to her, smiling. It could be a nice evening if she wasn't here against her will. She willingly grabs the sandwich and watches him as he starts making a second one. It is twice as big as his and he doesn't bother to cut the tomato or pickles properly. He wolfs down the last piece of his sandwich as she begins eating the second half of hers.

"What do you want to drink?" He opens the fridge wide and starts listing all the available beverages, "White wine, rosé, water, beer, coke, orange soda, lemonade..."

"Water," she interrupts.

"You sure?" he asks, his eyes darting to her.

She changes her mind. After all, this delicious meal would go perfectly with wine. "I'll have a glass of white."

"Me too." He takes out the bottle and fills two glasses. Then, he lifts his glass up in the air for a toast and gulps it all down. She is just finishing her sandwich, and takes a few sips from her glass.

"I'm going to ask Friz if he can go to your place and bring back some of your stuff." Without waiting for her to answer, he calls his friend. "He'll be here soon. Do you have your keys? An address?"

"I'd like to go with."

"That's impossible, you can't dematerialize." She gives in and hands him her set of keys before telling him her address. As she does so, Friz walks into the room. He materializes in the entrance hall. He looks hard at the human girl who is just finishing her glass of wine and then shakes his head, his gaze directed at Slash. The latter does his best to ignore it as he hands him Camilla's keys and address.

"I'll be quick," Friz declares before disappearing.

"He scares me," Camilla admits.

"He's not the worst of them."

No. That would be Viper. He scared the hell out of her when he stood up to bare her teeth at her at *Byzance*. She takes the sponge from the edge of the sink and starts wiping bread crumbs off the high table. Suddenly, she can feel Slash's presence behind her.

"You smell good, Camilla."

Her perfume? Her blood? Maybe both. He moves closer.

"What perfume do you wear?" he asks, brushing her hair off her neck. He bends forward and breathes her in. She smells like cinnamon.

"I don't wear any perfume."

"Then it is your blood that must smell of cinnamon." He tilts his head to one side before putting his lips onto her neck. Her skin is as soft as a newborn's; its smell reminds him of peaches. His body seems really attracted to that woman... so much so that he forgets about the most important thing in his long life: his punishment. "You smell of peaches, too."

"That's my shower gel."

She can feel Slash's lips brush across the nape of her neck. It is a delicious but dangerous sensation. She cannot forget who he is. That being said, his lips and his breath on her skin are starting to make her feel a bit feverish and desire wakes inside of her. A question pops up into her mind and she asks, "Can vampires sleep with humans? I mean... without hurting them."

"Of course. Vampires aren't monsters, we can be very gentle. Look, I'll show you." He lays a soft kiss on her neck... and then peppers a few deeper kisses on her throat, adding a bit of tongue to make them more sensual. He wraps his arms around Camilla, pressing her against his erection. He abandons her neck and easily finds her mouth as she turns her head to face him. He first kisses her with self-restraint before slipping his tongue into her mouth while his right hand moves up her thigh, reaching the lingerie under her skirt. He strokes a finger across her wetness.

She wants him.

He makes his way past the fabric and easily slides his fingers inside of her, wiggling them as they share another passionate kiss. They stay in that position for a few minutes, forgetting that Friz might teleport himself into the room at any time. Slash pulls his fingers out of her and turns her around so she can face him. He first presses her against him, kissing her feverishly, and then sits her down on the table, pulling her against his turgescent shaft. He feels like the buttons on his pants are about to burst open! A vibration. A vibration inside his jeans. Damn! His phone. He takes a step backwards, leaving Camilla with his smell imprinted on her and very frustrated.

"Yes, Kral."

"*Is the human girl with you?*"

"Yes, she's here."

"*Get both yours butts over here, right now.*"

"Okay, we'll be there in a minute. Are you at your place?"

"*Of course!*"

Slash puts the phone back in his pocket and tells Camilla about his short conversation with Kraler. Grabbing her by the hips, he puts her back on her feet. She smoothes down her skirt as Friz suddenly materializes into the kitchen, an overnight bag in his hands. He shoots a glance at Slash, shakes his head and puts the suitcase on the floor before throwing the keys at him. Slash catches them on the fly. "That's a very stupid thing you're doing, buddy!"

Turning a deaf ear, Slash doesn't reply as he gives Camilla her keys back.

"You'll regret this!" Friz adds. His friend's indifference is irritating him.

"I don't have time for this, Friz! Kraler is waiting for me."

"You've been warned!" shouts the blond vampire, bolting out in a flash. Slash spins around and stares at the young woman apprehensively. He has no idea what she might be feeling right now.

"What did he mean by that?"

"The room reeks of sex."

"That doesn't answer my question."

"Kraler is waiting for us..."

"Slash," she interrupts him, putting a hand on his arm.

He can feel the heavy sexual tension in the room. She is still hungry for more and full of desire for him. He knows that if he slipped his hand between her thighs, he would feel her warmth, but Friz is right. It is a very stupid thing to do. She is the girlfriend of a soldier who was sent to kill him, but that's not only problem... How will he manage to back out now that he has touched her?

"Seriously, Camilla. Kral doesn't like to wait."

CHAPTER 18

Kraler is pacing in his living room, wearing out another carpet. He asked Slash to bring the human girl over here fifteen minutes ago, what the hell is he doing? He only lives a five minutes ride away! Kraler is seething. Angel should wake up soon according to Slater Lawson – their doctor – who just left. He would like Camilla to be there when she does. That way she would understand that he means her no harm.

For God's sake, what the hell is Slash doing?

He keeps on pacing across the large living room. At least his place is spacious enough, not like Angel's house where he can't even move his feet without bumping into the furniture. Kral loves big spaces, he needs to be able to move freely, otherwise he feels smothered and becomes irritated and violent. Usually, being in his living room appeases him but if Slash doesn't show up soon, he's going to go mad.

In an attempt to cool off, he goes into his room where Angel is still fast asleep, looking peaceful under his black, silk bedsheets. He wishes he could have spent the previous day sleeping next to her instead of on the couch. He could have touched her, breathe in her perfume. He approaches her and gazes down at her relaxed face. It won't stay that way, surely enough. He squats down, putting his hand on her cheek and stroking it gently but a knock on the door interrupts him.

As his eyes flick to the hallway, he senses that Slash and the human girl have arrived. He exits the room, gently closing the door behind him before rushing to the front foor and pulling it open. His sense of smell is unerring. Slash and Angel's friends are here.

"Took you a hell of a while!" he growls, stepping to the side to let them in.

"Is she awake?" Slash wonders.

"Not yet."

Slash unties Camilla's blindfold, who then gazes around the apartment, wondering what it is about vampires and large places. "It's spacious," she notes.

"Kral can't bear being cramped," Slash explains.

Kraler stares at him in disbelief. Why the fuck are they making small talk?

"Where's Angel?" Camilla asks impatiently.

"Take it easy, human!" Kraler barks.

"Camilla." She stares at him, waiting for his answer. Slash regrets not telling her she should stay calm and polite with their leader if she doesn't want to suffer a horrible death.

"Lower your gaze!" he demands. His tone is ice cold and his predatory gaze makes her shiver.

"I'm sorry," she mumbled, looking down. He scares her now. Slash keeps silent, which leads Camilla to believe that he fears Kraler even more when he is angry.

"We'll discuss your case later. What you're going to do now is go to Angel's room and wait for her to wake up," he says in a threatening voice.

"Where's the room?"

After asking Slash to wait for him here, Kral takes Camilla to his room. Angel is still sleeping. "She's been sedated but it shouldn't be long before she opens her eyes." His menacing expression eases into a softer one as he gazes lovingly at Angel.

David is right. He is in love with her.

The realization that he would never do anything to hurt her strikes her suddenly. But then, why did he lose control and...? "Why did you try to bite her?"

His gaze flicks from Angel to Camilla. How dare she! "That is none of your business." Storming out of the room, he joins Slash back in the living room. "I need you to go to Angel's house and bring back some of her stuff."

"Now?"

"Please."

"What about... Camilla?"

Kraler detects a flicker of worry in his friend's eyes. "It's not the right time to talk about her case," he says, staring at Slash who looks slightly embarrassed. "Don't tell me you have a thing for her!"

"She gave me a hard-on."

"Slash, come the fuck on!"

"If you hadn't called me I... She wanted it so bad, man! I couldn't control myself." Slash is harsh on himself and regrets not managing to keep his cool. How could he be so stupid? He cant have sexual intercourse! The word sex is excluded from his vocabulary! Forever. He is well aware of that fact and he promises himself he won't ever get close to that human again.

95

"She can't stay at your place."

"I can't leave her at the manor. Viper might try and show her what it's like to get it hard! Well... you know him. I can't leave her there."

"Friz or Dark could keep an eye on her."

"Dark will try to pervert her and she doesn't like Friz."

"Slash, she can't stay with you!"

"Leave it, Kral. I'll just bite the bullet and and I swear it won't happen again."

"It better not! Because we don't know what we're going to do about her yet and we'll take a decision tonight."

"Kral, please."

"Bring me back some of Angel's stuff, I want her to feel safe when she wakes up."

Slash nods and disappears.

Fucking hell!

Kraler doesn't know how he's going to sort out that problem yet, but he is definitely going to find a way. Slash can't give in to that human, it would be much too serious. He hasn't had sex with a woman in almost a century. He is forbidden from having intercourse with female humans.

Slash materializes into Angel's house – it feels safe. No soldier around. He looks for her room and an overnight bag, which he fills with the kind of clothes that seem necessary and some toiletries. He doesn't know the first thing about women but he usually spends hours in the bathroom getting ready, so he knows what she is going to need.

He quickly goes around the house and takes in the broken table in the kitchen. A fight with Kraler? Only he could do such a thing! He leans against the door frame as a cinnamon smell tickles his nose. Camilla's perfume is all over the place. She probably visits Angel quite often. The image of their bodies pressed against one another flashes in his mind. What the hell was he thinking? Jesus! The thought gives him a hard-on. It is *so* not the right moment. He grits out a swearword between his teeth. The damn human girl for turning him on so badly. If it wasn't for Kraler's call, he might have made the second worst mistake of his life. The consequences would have been terrible. How could he have forgotten? If he doesn't manage to suppress his fricken erection, he's going to need to use the bathroom. Camilla. Her cinnamon smell. *Shit! That's not gonna help.* Goddammit! She was wet, ready to receive him. He takes his fingers to his nose, the smell of her juices still imprinted on them.

He closes his eyes and breathes in her odor, feeling his sex getting even harder. He swears again.

Left with no other choice, he goes up to the bathroom. He hasn't touched a female or even had an erection in decades. Nothing turned him on anymore. Nothing until now. He unzips his pants, releasing his shaft, which hasn't given him pleasure in such a long time. Unsure about whether he still knows how to do it, he wraps his hand around it and starts pleasuring himself. What he shouldn't have done is think about Camilla as a surge of ntense pleasure rushes through him, unloading his fluids in the toilet bowl. It isn't enough. He is still horny. He comes several times before his arousal finally turns off. He washes his hands in the marble sink and casts an automatic glance at the oval mirror. A disfigured man with a scar on his left cheek stares back at him. That's how it all began.

It was dark and he had just come out of his parents' house, intending to join his friend Rese. They often went from bar to bar, finding females to have some fun with females. In those times, it didn't matter whether they were vampires or humans because there wasn't much difference. The only thing is that with humans, sex was better as they would drain their blood upon reaching climax. An indescribable pleasure, albeit a one-sided one.

They were young and carefree.

Up until the day Slash had sex with one particular human girl. She was incredibly beautiful, young and attractive. She'd been glancing at him all night. He was handsome back then, his face scarless. Rese was there, trying to persuade him to buy a drink to the lady, so he'd listened to his friend and had started for the counter. They'd talked for a bit and then he'd taken her to the hotel, as he did with almost all the girls he met in those times, nearly a century ago. They'd had sex then and she was quite a demanding sex-partner. He still remembers. In fact, he was never able to forget her or even that damned night.

As he was reaching climax, he had sunk his teeth into her throat and sucked all of her blood. How immensely pleasurable! How wonderful it had felt! How powerful her life force had been! He hadn't even withdrawn from his victim yet when the door swung open. A man was there, a dagger in his hand. He hadn't immediately understood what was happening. The man had lunged at him and slashed his face. Slash was already a Snake at the time and his sword was lying on his bedside table. He had reached for it in a flash to defend himself against the angry vampire.

There had been no winner; the man had given up the fight to focus on the girl's lifeless body. Slash didn't understand anything at first but some time later he found out the girl he had killed was the partner of a powerful vampire.

Armus: a Snake warrior. Slash had felt miserable upon hearing the news. He had killed the companion of one of his brothers. Kraler was already lead at that time and Slash had been severely punished.

Reluctantly, Kral had sentenced him to a hundred whip lashes, etching the skin on his back forever, but it hadn't been enough for Slash who wanted to be sure he would never again make such a mistake. In front of the whole vampire assembly, he had vowed to never touch a female again. He had even made Kraler swear that he would cut off his private parts should he ever break that pledge. The leader of the pack had protested, unwilling to do such a thing if Slash was to give in to his male instincts someday but the latter had then asked Armus to make him that promise. Kraler had interposed himself and finally accepted the deal.

In order to make sure he would never fail his word, Slash had also forbidden himself from drinking a woman's blood. He had become a sort of vampire monk.

But Camilla! Nobody had ever had such an effect on him!

CHAPTER 19

Angel opens her eyes, feeling as if she has been sleeping for days. There is enough light in the room for her to see but she has no idea where she is.

"Angel."

She recognizes Camilla's voice and turns her head to look at her friend. It's so good to see her! She smiles.

"How do you feel?"

"Good."

Camilla gives her a soft look. For a fleeting moment, she thought her friend might never come round.

"Where are we?"

"At Kraler's."

Memories of what happened in her house flash in Angel's mind. She wanted him to make love to her and he wanted to drink her blood. She had said no and he had literally lunged at her. She lays her hand on her throat but feels nothing unusual there.

"It's faded off," Camilla tells her.

Angel tries to remember what happened after the bite but nothing comes to mind except for the shock she had felt. A breathtaking feeling of shock. "What happened?"

"I don't know. You're gonna have to ask Kraler."

"He wanted to drink my blood!" she snarls.

"I don't know that either. He didn't want to talk to me."

"Is he here?"

"With Slash."

"What are *you* doing here?"

"I was worried about you so I went to Byzance, hoping to find Kraler. I'll spare you the details for now, but since I'm dating a soldier, they've decided to keep me."

"Are you their prisoner or something?" Angel's eyes widen.

"I'm staying at Slash's. I guess you could say I'm a prisoner, yes. I also know that Kraler is going to decide what they're gonna do about me."

"Nonsense! Go and get him for me! I'm going to tell him what's on my mind exactly!"

"Forget it. You should relax a little and think. I believe he loves you."

"You're going crazy!"

"Look, I probably shouldn't tell you but he'd like you to become his partner."

"He can keep on dreaming!" This all seems like a horrible nightmare. She is trapped in a vampire's house who wants to marry her when he nearly killed her.

"Do you want to have a shower?" Camilla suggests.

"Are you fucking kidding me? I want to get out of here!" Angel tries to get up but Camilla stops her.

"You're not going anywhere!"

"Did he hypnotize you too?"

"I don't know what you're talking about."

As she lifts up the blanket, Angel notes that she is only wearing a T-shirt – which doesn't even belong to her. Kraler must have undressed her.

"I don't know what happened, but... I know that..."

"What? Camilla!"

"You had a heart attack."

Angel's eyes pop out. "I had a shock." She remembers the ordeal she went through, the smothering feeling as if her whole body was lacking in oxygen, the burning sensation in her organs. She could have died because of him but she had a heart attack. How can... "Who resuscitated me?"

"I don't know but when the soldiers and I walked in, Slash was near you and you were conscious."

"Meaning that Slash must have saved me...?" The scary guy with the scar? Impossible!

"I'll see if I can get you some clothes. You should have a shower in the meantime."

Angel nods in agreement as Camilla heads out of the room. A stroke! Lord... she could be dead now. If it wasn't for that damn vampire!

She gets up effortlessly and walks across the bright and spacious bedroom. It's the same size as the ground floor in her house! She opens the door to her left, the bathroom - which is as big as her own bedroom. Seems like that vampire is a bit megalomaniac! He apparently thinks on a big scale.

Angel slips into the - big enough for several people - shower stall and turns on the hot water. She needs it. Everything falls into place in her head; she replays what could have been her last day on earth in her mind and shudders. Slash had saved her life. He had bent over her when she suddenly sat up straight to take a deep breath and asked her if she was okay several times. Then there had been Camilla and the soldiers, with David taking aim at Slash. Kraler telling her friend to back off, his arms lifting her up. The soldiers leaving as she watched helplessly. She had sort of felt absent, under the shock and powerless.

Kraler took her here, flanked by all the other vampires. She'd been examined by a doctor, so it seemed, and then... That's all. The rest is blurry.

"Excuse me," Camilla speaks softly as she steps into the living room where Kraler is still pacing. "Is Slash around?"

"He'll be back soon."

"Would you happen to have any of Angel's stuff?"

"Is she awake?"

"Yes."

A smile creeps across the vampire's face. Finally! He's going to see her, explain her what happened and maybe hold her close against him – he needs it so badly. What he craves even more badly is her forgiveness because he feels terribly guilty.

Before either of them can open their mouth again, Slash materializes in the room, holding two suitcases. He drops them to the floor, looking tormented and avoiding Camilla's gaze.

"You okay, man?" Kral worries, sensing Slash's awkwardness.

The latter finds it impossible to reply anything; his throat is completely blocked.

"Bring these to Angel," Kraler orders Camilla.

She takes a step towards Slash in order to grab the suitcases. He doesn't look at her and moves away a little. She doesn't understand what's going on but she walks out of the room and up the stairs, obeying Kral.

"I jerked off thinking about her... and not just once!"

Kral senses how troubled his friend is. He also knows how things might deteriorate if Slash doesn't control himself: he risks getting emasculated.

"I'm going to let her go," Kral decides. "If I keep her here, Angel will be mad at me and you'll have to fight temptation on a daily basis. If I kill her, my relationship will get even worse."

Slash nods in agreement, unable to pronounce a single word.

"Did she leave any of her stuff at your place?"

Again, Slash uses his head to answer.

"I'm going to ask Friz to bring them over here. As for you, you're going to go back to the manor and chill out."

Slash gives Kral a grateful look before disappearing. The leader picks up his phone from the table in the living room and calls Friz, asking him to go to Slash's and bring the human girl's things over here.

Camilla puts the suitcases down in the bedroom, thinking worriedly about Slash's obvious uneasiness. She imagines that he must have had an argument with Kraler. What else could it be? She will end up finding out since they will go back home together. Feeling reassured, she smiles. And suddenly, the memory flashes in her mind: he was avoiding *her* gaze. His awkwardness wasn't due to Kraler's presence but to her own. What has she done for him to act that way towards her? In any case, she will find out soon enough. They've pretty much kidnapped her and Slash is supposed to keep an eye on her, isn't he? Angel comes out of the bathroom, wearing only a towel around her chest.

"I have some of your clothes," Camilla declares.

Slash hits the punch bag as hard as he can. He uses it to cool off too. Running on the treadmill or lifting weights doesn't help him relax but boxing is a good way to let the steam off. He enjoys it just as much as Kraler. He forces Camilla out of his thoughts. Why the hell did he have to meet that human? He doesn't believe in destiny. People decide what life they want to lead and make their own choices, nothing is pre-written. He had never looked at a female in the way he looked at Camilla back when they were at his place. Maybe that was the moment it had all clicked into place, in the kitchen.

He throws blow after blow but try as he might, he can't seem to relax and let go of his irritation. He is angry at himself for being so weak after a whole year of abstinence. His only consolation being that he might never see her again. Kraler is going to release her. That doesn't mean he'll be able to erase her from his memory though. It's too late for that, it should have been done before. However, the vampires' existence isn't a secret anymore, Camilla isn't a threat to his race. She'll just go back to her life, with the soldier. She won't try and see him again so he doesn't have to worry about that. A few days from now, everything will be back to normal for sure.

He focuses on his training, feeling the tension ease little by little. He can't let himself think of anything else. He needs to empty his mind. Forget everything. It's important, otherwise he won't be able to get any rest.

Friz appears in Kraler's living room. The latter is staring out the window, taking in the darkness of the night and the city lights through the huge glass wall; the view is breath-taking. Kral's apartment is on the 20th floor of a tower. His vision is so acute he can see *Byzance* down in the street and the crowd standing in line in the hope of making it to the doors. No human could see that from where he is standing.

"Kral?"

The lead swings around to face Friz. "I didn't hear you. Have you..." he breaks off, glancing down at the bag lying on the floor, answering his question.

"So what about the human girl?"

"I'm going to release her. It won't do any good to keep her here against her will."

"That's the right thing to do."

Kraler is surprised. He was expecting Friz to object: Camilla's link with the soldiers could be useful for them. They could have used her as bait. That's the kind of arguments he was expecting to hear from his friend's mouth.

"Slash is going out of control, Kral."

So he's noticed it too. Kraler nods his head. "I know."

"When I got there, in his apartment... it smelt of sex."

"That's why he's not in charge of her anymore. You'll take her back home."

"Now?"

"Why waste any time, I need to speak with my future wife."

Friz smiles. He's never heard these words come out of Kraler's mouth. The idea of their leader falling for a woman, a human one at that, is just bewildering and unexpected.

"I'll bring her back here," Kraler declares before dashing upstairs and knocking on his bedroom door.

Angel just finished getting dressed; she is now wearing jeans and a sweater. There's no way she was going to put on a dress or a skirt, especially since she knows she's going to have to confront Kraler. Her eyes dart to the door as someone raps on it three times.

"Camilla, please, can you come out?" Kral demands.

Recognizing the vampire's voice, Angel's heart leaps inside her chest. She glances at Camilla.

"I'll be right back," her friend promises.

Angel goes to the bathroom and starts brushing her hair while Camilla exits the bedroom. Although she expected to find Slash in the living room, it is Friz who is waiting for her.

"Where's Slash?"

"At the manor."

Kraler takes a few steps forwards to face her, towering above her. "Friz is going to take you back home."

"I've already left some of my stuff at Slash's."

"Your stuff is here," he cuts off, pointing at the bag next to her feet.

"I don't understand" she says to Kraler.

"We're not keeping you here any longer, you can finally go back home."

That's good news. Well, she thinks. She was hoping she could talk to Slash about what was wrong but that'll have to wait. She'll try and find him at *Byzance* one of these nights.

"Fine," she snaps.

"One last thing before you go – you can't hang round any of us."

"Of course not."

"Slash included. Especially Slash." Kraler's tone is cold and menacing, making his words an order. Camilla burns to find out why but she won't ask him the question. His predatory gaze terrifies her and her inner voice advises her to keep her mouth shut. She cannot defy him or disrespect him. She is perfectly aware of who she is facing. A vampire.

"Friz, take the human back home. Blindfold her."

The blond vampire nods and wraps a black scarf around Camilla's head. He picks up her bag, flings it over his shoulder and pulls Camilla by the arm. She keeps silent and obediently follows the man she doesn't like.

Kraler fixes his stare on the window again, walking towards it until his forehead touches the cold glass. *How beautiful!* He takes a deep breath. It's time for them to talk. He can feel her, she is so close.

CHAPTER 20

Angel steps into the spacious living room she has never seen before. She is sure of one thing: Kraler has very good taste. The furniture is sophisticated, the colors sober. Nothing is gaudy or useless. Her eyes scan the room and finally meet his silhouette in front of the huge bay windows. A feeling of dizziness spreads through her. It's so high! She couldn't get as close to the window as him. "Kral?" she calls.

He turns around to look at her, thinking how perfect she is in her skin-tight jeans and close-fitting sweater.

"Where's Camilla?"

"Friz took her back home."

"I thought you were holding her hostage."

"Not anymore."

A surge of relief washes over her. He could have given up his hopes to talk to her if he'd hurt her friend in any way. She stands at the back of the room, not only because of her fear of heights but also because she hasn't forgotten their last moment together. What he did to her is etched in her memory. She is angry at him and intends to let him know exactly how she feels. Even if he's a vampire. Even if he terrifies her. Once she is done with him, he won't dare to get close to her ever again. That being said, at this very moment, he looks uncomfortable rather than scary. *Wait for it, buddy! I'm going to make you regret even being born!* "I would like to thank Slash."

"What for?"

"Saving my life. After you abandoned my corpse!" she snarls.

"I didn't know... and I was ashamed." He stands motionless, facing the window, his voice incredibly calm. He needs to control himself and bite the bullet if he wants her forgiveness.

"I remember everything." She takes a step in his direction, and then another. She wants to get closer and yell at him, make him understand that she isn't scared of him and hates what he has done to her. "I had forbidden you to drink my blood!" she growls. "You must be some kind of animal, disrespecting the woman you say you love!"

The words stab him right in the heart, making him dangerously lose his cool.

"I don't know why you brought me back here and—"

"To take care of you," he interrupts her, trying not to raise his voice too much.

It kind of makes sense now that she thinks about it. She actually feels bad for not realizing it earlier.

"I regret what I've done! Okay? I really regret it!" he admits louder. He is angry but Angel understands that his anger is not directed at her, but at himself. "Here's what's in my heart: I'm ashamed of myself." His voice is low now and he turns around to face the darkness so she can't see his face.

He's ashamed of himself! Bet he is! Nothing seems to appease Angel's anger. "You killed me! If it wasn't for Slash's intervention, I'd be dead now!" she yells.

"I wish you would forgive me."

"In your dreams! You can forget about me!"

That stabbing feeling strikes again. He is finding it more and more difficult to keep his cool. He knows he will explode if she keeps on hurting him like this – deliberately, at that.

"I want to go home!"

"I want you to stay here."

"I won't stay here another minute! You're just a blood-thirsty monster! Ready to suck your girlfriend's blood! You're disgusting!"

"Enough!" He leaps towards her, now only a few inches from that body he desires so and which she refuses to let him have. "You can't say these things to me... I'm sorry."

She is perfectly aware of the pain she is inflicting on him but her anger at him won't fade the slightest bit. He nearly killed her for God's sake! Without thinking, she slaps him. It helps her calm down. But the dark, menacing spark in his eyes make her swallow. Maybe she shouldn't have done that.

"Don't you ever lay your hands on me again. I could kill you for what you just did."

His coldness scares her to death. He just lost control and that's the last thing he wanted but she provoked him for her own amusement! You don't push Kraler to the edge without facing the consequences!

"Is that how you feel about me?" Unable to hold back her tears any longer, she lets them roll down her cheeks. He has gone too far. Again! Letting go of her, he takes two steps backwards. breathing slowly, which helps him calm down almost instantly.

"No, of course not." He starts pacing the room. "I didn't expect our conversation to take this turn. I was obviously prepared to face your resentment but what I wasn't prepared for were your hurtful, offensive words. I can't control myself when I get so deeply hurt."

Angel peels herself off the wall and runs a hand through her hair. Okay, maybe she was a bit cruel but her words are justified and he doesn't seem to understand that.

"I thought... I was hoping you'd understand my point of view, that you'd let me explain what happened. I never thought you'd scathe me like that."

"I almost died," she explains.

"I know that. I made a mistake, but I made up for it."

"What was it that you wanted to explain to me?"

He doesn't look at her, his gaze fixed on the starry night which seems to draw him. "I have very strong urges when I'm with you. Sexual urges, obviously, but your blood is very appealing too. My feelins for you aren't separated from these desires, they are entirely related to them. The ultimate orgasm for a vampire is to take possession of the body of the female he loves at the same time that he drinks her blood. I wanted to achieve that with you," he says, turning around to meet her eyes. "I want to share everything with you. I want our blood to mingle, for you to taste mine while I taste yours. I'm not sure whether you truly comprehend what I'm telling you. It might sound ridiculous to you because you're not part of my world but I want you. I love you, undoubtedly. Forgive me for losing control, it won't happen again." He just poured his heart out to her, that's the most he can do. If she doesn't understand him, he'll die. He will become but a mere shadow of himself, he knows it deep down.

Angel heard him. Understanding him is another matter. She is aware that their two races have different customs but it doesn't excuse his animal-like ways towards her. "It will definitely never happen again. I've listened to you, that's what you wanted. I'm even going to apologize for the slap – I shouldn't have. But don't ask for more. I want to go back home and get my life back... without you."

Her words stab through his heart a third time.

He has lost her.

Angel grabs her bags from the bedroom. She hadn't emptied them. As if! She dashes back to the living room. Kraler is still standing in front of the windows, gazing out at the darkness. She starts for the door half-heartedly, thinking that he will probably materialize in front of it before she can run away but no, he remains motionless as she reaches the knob. She closes the door behind her. He doesn't even materialize on the landing. She takes the elevator which carries her down the twenty floors.

The vampire doesn't protest as she leaves the building. She feels lost but realizes quickly that she recognizes the street. Kraler lives right across Byzance. She looks up at the immense tower. A feeling of dizziness prickles at her spine. Can he see her from up there? She doesn't know. She will do him a favor though: she won't tell anybody where he lives. Despite everything that happened, she still loves him. Even if he's dangerous. She loves him.

Making her way through the crowd, she heads back home.

Kraler watches Angel as she disappears around the corner of the street.

What a douchebag!

How could he be so stupid and lose control? Why didn't he find the right words? She kindled so many things in him but he wasn't able to shut off his animal instincts.

Stupid predator!

His nature made him lose the one and only woman he loves. How ironic. Especially for someone who used to take lives without feeling the faintest hint of regret! Life is taking its revenge on him.

You declared war on me! Just wait and see how I'm going to retaliate!

Enough with the self-pity.

Enough with those feelins of love inside his heart.

Kraler just took a decision which might ensue major consequences. It is time to go to the secret Snake temple, time to check on all those young vampire warriors who have been training, time to blow up the military base.

He walks towards the square mirror hanging on the wall and takes off his shirt. He looks at the tattoo that covers his whole back: a black snake, its tongue sticking out of its mouth.

He's a Snake.

A warrior who was chosen to protect his race. It's about time he remembers that and stop going from bar to bar with his four peers.

He grabs his phone. "Viper, I want everyone at the manor in a half-hour."

"Okay, boss. Consider it done."

CHAPTER 21

It's only a few minutes walk home from Kraler's apartment, so Angel doesn't really have the time to wonder whether he is following her through the dark streets of the south district. She comes across several vampires who simply stare at her, without showing any intention to attack her. Might be a bit late for dinner! Making fun of the situation helps her calm down – which isn't an easy thing to do: a blood-thirsty predator nearly killed her! She doesn't pay any more attention to the people she walks by, her mind is replaying the words Kral told her, what he said about wanting her to be come his partner according to their vampiric traditions. He wants to drink her blood and for her to drink his. The very thought of this makes her sick. That being said, she has to admit that the sensation must be orgasmic. Exchanging that fluid essential to life with the one you love must feel... She could slap herself for having such ridiculous thoughts! He almost killed her once, she won't let him come near her ever again.

Angel doesn't have time to cool off before walking through the door. She is still as angry at the vampire and at his lack of self-control. Her irritation is so deep she feels as if she won't ever be able to forgive him. Her eyes immediately flick to the damned broken table in the kitchen. It reminds her of Kral's strength and violence, which comforts her in her decision. There is nothing to regret. He isn't right for her.

It is quite late and she is supposed to work tomorrow. She'll never manage to wake up! Well, it's not like she has a choice. She drops the bags in the hallway and goes to lie down on her bed. She doesn't relax as quickly as she thought she would but eventually drifts off to sleep.

The tension is palpable in the manor as Kraler starts speaking. The vampires can sense his intense irritation. He seems as if he is just about to explode.

109

"Brothers, it is time for us to take things in hand. I've had enough of those soldiers, enough of this life. Let's blow everything up!

Slash understands that Angel has left. Otherwise, Kral never would have mentioned that he was tired of his life. He never would have decided to take immediate action against the military men. It sounds obvious that he wants to make war.

"It's too late to do something tonight but as soon as the sun sets tomorrow, we'll go to the temple," Kraler goes on.

"To the temple?" Viper is surprised by this decision. They haven't been there in years. They've always managed the soldiers by themselves.

"It's about time I stop spending my nights drinking and fucking all the bitches in this neighborhood. I want to lead you and all the Snakes on the path to peace, because we all know we deserve it!"

"Are you thinking of extending the group?" Dark wonders.

"Not us. I'm the lead, you're the Council and they will be the warriors. It's about time everything falls into place."

"How are you going to get them all tattooed?" Friz asks. Every Snake warrior has a tattoo. If Kral decides to set up an army, it won't be very discreet to take all the guys to the Seattle tattoo parlors at once.

"A snake on the bicep will be enough. From now on, the one on our backs will be reserved to the members of the Council and myself. I'll leave it to you to find a few tattoo artists for tomorrow evening, then we'll erase their memories."

They nod.

"What do you intend to do?" Slash stares at him, waiting for an answer. He probably won't talk about the fact that the human girl left him and refused to become his partner.

"We're going to blow up the nearby military base."

"Finally!" Viper exclaims excitedly. "Glad you're back, man."

"It was time," Dark adds.

"They'll probably retaliate after that and declare war, which I hope they will. Or else, they'll leave us alone for good."

"A war! We're finally gonna smash their faces!"

Viper jubilates at the news; his desire to slaughter the soldiers is so strong he will kill any of thel who stands in his way. He's not the only one who is happy about Kraler's radical decision. Slash thinks it could help him keep his mind off Camilla. When everything is back to normal... a few months from now, he imagines his interest in her will have faded off completely. He will be free again.

110

The other guys, who always appreciate a good hunt, are also quite satisfied with the plan. *Byzance* and the entertainment they find there isn't enough anymore. They need adrenaline. They can already picture themselves diving in the bloodbath the explosion of the military base will be.

"Let's all meet here tomorrow as soon as the sun's down. We'll take two cars and drive all the way to the temple. I'll tell Yassin about our arrival."

"How about the tattoo artists?"

"Find some now and persuade them to go to the martial arts center tomorrow at dusk."

"Consider it done!"

Viper is the first one to exit the manor, flanked by Dark and Friz. Slash runs his hands across the table and paces the room.

"Got a problem?" Kraler asks him.

"I'm fine. You?"

"Fine too."

"Look, Kral... I don't wanna sound overly curious or anything but... How did it go with your human girl?"

"She didn't understand a single thing. I think..." he breaks off and takes a few steps across the huge room in the middle of which stands a big oak table. "She isn't worthy of me."

"Do you intend to see her again?"

"She has taken her decision and I respect it. I won't see her again and everything I just said during the meeting is a consequence of her leaving. I shall not wait at Byzance with my arms crossed. I'm going to take action because... because something has to be done. I have no other choice."

"That kind of thing leaves a hole in your heart, I understand it perfectly. You need to fill that hole in order to forget and move on." Slash puts a sympathetic hand on the giant's shoulder before walking out of the room.

That kind of thing leaves a hole in your heart. You need to fill that hole in order to forget and move on.

Slash gets him. Kraler realizes that. He believed in Angel's feelings towards him so much. He was almost certain she would understand things if he explained them clearly to her. She may have listened to him but she didn't want to hear. To think of how ridiculous he must have looked in front of his friends... He had made it clear he wanted to make this female his partner. After his speech about blowing up the base tomorrow, they must have realized that he had given up on her.

Jesus Christ! So fucking embarrassing!

111

He slams his fist on the table to evacuate some of his anger. There's nothing to do. The thought of her will never leave him. He could relieve himself a bit by finding another female but he feels no desire to do so. Even the thought of fucking some girl against a wall – which he really enjoys – doesn't turn him on. Pulling his phone out of the inside pocket of his long black coat, he dials Yassin's number.

"What an honor, my Lord!"

"Alright Yassin, no need to brown-nose me now!"

"How can I help you?"

"I will come to the temple at dusk tomorrow with the Countil. I want you to get your best warriors ready to join the Snakes."

"What an honor! It will be done, for sure."

"I shall then tell them about their mission and they will receive the sacred symbol of their affiliations to our family."

"Thank you, my Lord. I thought you were no longer interested in my institute."

"It's time for soldiers and humans to understand who the Snakes really are."

"I have more than four hundred warriors training here. They are all at your disposal."

"Thank you, Yassin. Also keep recruiting new men, I want more and more warriors. I want the Snakes to take on the whole city... for a start."

"What an honor!"

"See you tomorrow, Yassin."

"See you tomorrow, my Lord."

My Lord... my ass! He hates it when people call him that. It reminds him of who he is and everything he ran away from a few years earliers.

The leader of the Vampire clan.

They inherit this title from father to son.

After his father's death, Kraler was croned Lord of his race. At first, he was very serious about it but he slowly lost his interest. Half of his community wanted to live in harmony with humans and accepted to only feed off synthetic blood but he was against this alternative. It makes them lose their capacities, makes them less powerful. The soldiers knew what they were doing by giving them this only option so they could lead their live in peace. Kraler let them make their decision and led the way for all of those who had made the same choice as him but they all changed sides after a while and accepted to drink the fake blood to try and lead a better life.

Little by little, he got away from them. He created a club with the members of the vampire Council a.k.a the Judges, as they used to call themselves decades ago. At the time, Slash had just replaced Harim, an ancient vampire killed by military men.

Kraler feels that getting back to work after so many years will help him appease some of his rage. She doesn't want the predatory animal that he is. The monster. Well, she's in for a big surprise. This mission will be like a therapy for him, a way to exorcise that female from his heart, from his body and from his soul.

He had somehow become more human, living amongst men for such a long time, but it's over now. The beast inside of him wants to take over and he is going to let it take control. And those who stand in his way had better watch out.

It is time for him and for all the other vampires to show those humans that they are not their obedient little doggies.

CHAPTER 22

After work, Camilla decides to go and see David to get things straight with him. She hasn't taken the time to really ponder over her decision but since Slash has become an obsession, she can't imagine pursuing her relationship with the soldier.

She wants to break up.

She is perfectly aware that Kraler instructed her to stay away from the vampire but she doesn't plan on following the order and intends to go to *Byzance* this very evening to talk to him. From the moment he pressed his soft lips against the nape of her neck, she hadn't been able to think about anything else. She can still feel his ragged breath against her skin, his hands on her thighs, his fingers touching and then penetrating her lady parts. Nobody had ever made her feel that way before. She was eager to keep going and if it wasn't for Kraler's call, she would have made love with the vampire. She had a dream about it last night and it was amazing. She wants to fulfil that burning desire.

She knocks on the door of the apartment located downtown in a four-story building. Nothing. She knocks a bit louder. The door finally opens on a disheveled, unshaven and apparently sleepy David. "Camilla? Come on in." He yawns and ushers her into the messy living room. Empty beer cans and packets of crisps are scattered across the small table. Charming! She had no idea he was so untidy.

"I wasn't sure you'd be home at this hour of day."

He grabs a beer from the refrigerator and offers her one but she refuses. Seeing him like this doesn't soften her at all. It only confirms that she doesn't belong with a guy like him. Plus, she feels absolutely nothing for him. It is as if her feelings, once very strong, had entirely disappeared. Now there is only room for Slash in her heart. "Angel came back home last night. She's okay."

"How do you know?"

"She called me from work."

"Are you sure?"

114

"I'm not stupid! I'm going to see her later, actually."

"The vampires have released her, then."

"She had a heart attack. Kraler wanted to take care of her."

He gives a snicker. That confirms that the vampire leader is attracted to Angel. However, he doesn't feel like pondering that for the moment. He has something else on his mind. "I'd like to know if you're still mad at me."

"She didn't get back home thanks to you. If Kraler had wanted to hurt her, my friend would be dead now."

He swallows a few gulps of his beer. He knows that, of course. He's just a pathetic little soldier. He's aware of that. That's exactly why he hasn't gone to work since! He's a duffer! "So, in other words, yes, you are."

"I didn't only come here to tell you about Angel getting back home safe."

"What else did you want to tell me, then?"

"It's over."

"What is? What are you talking about?" A flick of fear flashes in his eyes. He is scared to understand what she means and doesn't think he will be able to handle it, especially not in the state he's in.

"Our *relationship* is over."

"All because of that stupid thing that happened!" he snarls.

"It's not just that. I need to distance myself from you."

"Like hell!" He drinks the rest of his bottle as she leaves. And as the door slams shut behind her, Camilla hears something smashing against it. David just threw his half-full beer at it. "Bitch!" he hisses between his teeth.

Angeline wonders if she will survive Camilla's visit. She doesn't know how she managed to stay awake all day but her sleep-deprived body is so weak she feels as if she is going to collapse at any moment.

She takes the easy option and decides to order dinner, feeling too exhausted to cook tonight. Camilla likes pizza, but as she might feel like eating something else for once, she decides against ordering. She pours herself a very strong cup of coffee, hoping it'll keep her awake at least another hour. There is a knock on the door as she takes a first sip. "Come in, Camilla."

The beautiful young woman walks in, beaming. Angel doesn't recall ever seeing her so happy... so radiant, even. "Wow! What's happening to you?" she asks, leaning against the kitchen counter, the steaming cup in her hand.

"You still haven't bought a new table!"

"I will tomorrow, normally. So?"

"I'm in love."

"Have you just been at David's?"

"Yes."

"It's obvious."

"Let me stop you right there. I broke up with him."

"Well you're going to have to explain that to me."

"That's what I'm here for. Have you cooked dinner yet?"

"No, I'm exhausted."

"Let's order. I'm starving."

She fumbles in the drawer where she keeps flyers and stuff and quickly goes through them. "Pizza?"

I knew it! She nods in agreement.

"Three-cheese?"

Smiling, she nods again. She knows her friend by heart. Not wasting a minute, she calls to order a three-cheese pizza and a ham, mushroom and mozarella one.

"So? How did it go with Kraler?" she asks after hanging up the phone.

"It's over."

"Your anger was stronger than your feelings."

"He wants things I cannot give him."

"Like your blood, I imagine."

"I'm not part of his world."

"So you left."

"Yes."

"He didn't try to hold you back?"

"He was looking through the bay windows but he didn't budge when I left. I was sure he'd fight for me but he didn't." She lifts the steaming cup to her lips and takes a slurp. It is difficult for her to speak about the end of her relationship with Kraler – even though it ended before it even had time to begin.

"Do you want a cup of coffee?" she offers her friend. She wants to stop talking about Kraler. It's no use anyway, it only hurts her more. It's over. Why keep speaking about it?

"No. I'm already feeling pretty overexcited!"

"I can see that." Angel looks completely worn out, in contrast.

"Something incredible happened when I was at Slash's."

"Meaning...?"

"He touched me in a way no man ever had. What I felt was... wow!"

"You had sex with Slash!" Angel cries, dumbfounded.

"No. Kraler had the great idea to call just as we were about to."

"So... are you going out with the vampire?"

"Not really. He's been acting weird ever since and Kraler told me to stay away from him."

"Surprising."

"I'm going to *Byzance* tonight."

"And I am so not coming with you."

"I can see that you're tired but... do you not wanna see Kraler?" she smiles mischeviously.

"I've broken up with him, Camilla."

"Don't you miss him?"

"I'm still angry. I'd be dead because of him if it wasn't for what Slash did!"

"What happened?"

"He wanted to drink my blood," she answers before taking another gulp of her coffee. "I said no but he couldn't hold back. I had a heart attack because of it. I can't forgive him what he did!" She puts the half-full cup in the sink. Camilla is asking her to recount a very painful memory and she doesn't particularly feel like reliving that moment. "Don't ever talk to me about him again," she demands, her hands clenching the sink. "I'm begging you, Camilla. I just want to... forget."

Camilla isn't stupid, she can sense the pain in her friend's voice but also her feelings towards Kraler, which are still strong and present despite what she told her. Once her anger has faded, she will most definitely crave him. The way she feels about him is certainly similar to the way she feels about Slash. It is like a fever. Irrevocable. Indescribable. Spellbinding. A burning desire. She won't be able to keep away from his body for a very long time. Camilla is already consumed with the craving feeling Slash left her with.

Dinner arrives promptly as Angel is a regular. They eat together in the living room – drinking rosé wine with the pizzas. Camilla does the talking. All she talks about is Slash. Angel understands the effect he has on her even if she is surprised that her friend got over David so quickly. It isn't like her.

The temple of martial arts. It has been such a long time since Kraler set foot in here. The view is unbelievable. The temple of the vampire warriors is perched on a high mountain. Nobody knows what happens behind those walls apart from them, the vampires. Everybody thinks it is a simple martial arts training center. Even the army thinks so. Nobody knows who Yassin really is. People come from very far to enrol their sons in that place.

Yassin only recruits vampires. He tells humans that they are already full or that they are going to put their child on a waiting list. Sometimes he even erases their memories so they don't remember ever coming here. The vampires who want to join the center train to become skilled warriors. He also erases the memory of those who are against the idea. Works every time. At least it has for the past decades.

Kraler gazes up at the huge steel gate in front of him. They are at least sixteen feet high. There is no way anyone can ever break into the temple. The whole center is encircled by a twenty feet high defensive wall. Impossible to get in. Impossible to get out.

The leader's eyes hold no hint of emotion as he walks forward imperturbably. He knocks on the huge gate that resonates at his touch. It slowly opens before him. His arrival was much awaited – it is an honor for the young warriors.

"My Lord," Yassin himself greets him, kneeling in front of him.

"Let's begin," Kral says in a cold, impassive tone.

Yassin is reunited with his leader, the head of the cold-blooded creatures. "My Lords," he greets the Snake Council.

The gate closes behind them and Yassin ushers them to the inner courtyard where all the warriors are waiting for them. The vampires step aside to let the leader flanked by his four friends climb on stage. Yassin planned everything in advance to make sure the night goes according to their leader's will. He even placed a microphone on the platform so that the whole audience can hear the sacred words of the vampire he considers as the chosen one. The one who will save them all.

Kraler is facing more than four hundred vampires. It is a bit intimidating but he doesn't let that unsettle him.

"Viper? The tattoo guys?"

"They are here, my Lord." He smiles and points at a group of about twenty men. *My Lord.* Nobody had called him that in a very long time, apart from Yassin, of course. And coming from Viper, it certainly means he has immense respect for what he is about to do. He's finally come to his senses, it was time!

"Vampires," Kral speaks, scanning over the assembly. "I have neglected my role for too long. Officially, I am resuming work right now. I'm going to tell the soldiers tomorrow. *We* are going to tell the soldiers tomorrow," he corrects himself, lifting up his arm.

They all imitate him, crying out their joy and devotion. They approve of him whole-heartedly!

"Yassin will choose the fifty best warriors among you to start with. The quickest ones with the sharpest sense of smell. That's very important if we want to see our terrorist action through to the end. Those fifty warriors will get a tattoo of a snake on their left bicep." He pauses for a moment, taking in their awe-struck expressions. It is an honor for a vampire to officially become a Snake. "At the end of the week, the military base three miles from the city I will live in soon will blow up. Thanks to you!" He points at them, adding to their excitement. The members of the Countil have to admit that he is still as charismatic as ever – he was born a leader. And he will be an exemplary one now that he feels strong enough to fight. They are all convinced of that. "The four members next to me, Friz, Dark, Slash and Viper make up the Council of the Snakes. You are to treat them with due respect. I'm now going to hand over to Viper, who will tell you more about tomorrow night."

Kraler steps back, letting his friend do the talking, only to happy to explain them all the details about the attack. He joins Yassin, eager to meet the fifty best applicants here and now.

At 10 o'clock on the dot, Camilla walks into Byzance alone. She tried to convince Angel to come along but her stubborn friend refused squarely. *We'll talk about it in a few days!* she had thought. She shots glances around the crowded room but cannot find the one she wants to see. She starts for the counter and orders a soda. The dark-haired barman smiles as he hands her her drink.

"Are you Stefan, by any chance?" she ventures. Angel mentioned him just before she let her leave. She thought he might be able to help if Slash wasn't around.

"Do I know you?" He stares at her but can't place her. How could he forget such a pretty face?

"I'm Angel's friend. She told me about you."

"Angel, I remember her. She didn't come with you?"

"Too tired to go out." She takes a sip of her soda before asking him if Slash might show up later.

"What do these guys have that I don't?" he says jokingly. "Your friend has the hots for Kral and you have the hots for Slash."

"Do you know if he'll show up?" she asks again, ignoring his remark.

"No idea, love. I haven't seen him tonight and I didn't see him yesterday either, for that matter."

"Any clue where I can find him?" He called her *love*. Might as well be as familiar with him as he is with her.

"Sorry. I'm not his father! Slash is a big boy!"

"I'll wait," she decides before gazing down at her drink.

Stefan watches her, smiling, and then goes to attend to his other customers.

The night seems promising for the vampires. Fifty of them just got a snake tattooed on their body. Those fifty guys are the ones who will participate in the attack. Kraler's eyes are ever so bright. He is back to his old, non-human self. They will use a bomb one of the vampire physicists is currently making. Watching him prepare gives him pleasure close to orgasm. How could he do without all this for so long? This euphoric feeling of power he gave up on just to try and live like a human, amongst other humans. A wave of excitement washes over his whole body, causing his muscles to contract. He gazes up at the sky before closing his eyes, relishing the feeling.

"If I was a female, I'd rub myself against our Lord," Viper jubilates.

"You're crazy!" Dark laughs.

"Do you think he might be interesed in a gay relationship?" The question was for Dark but all three of them burst out laughing. That's the best joke they've heard in decades. "I'm serious guys! I'm loving the boss tonight!"

They break into loud guffaws again.

"What's so funny?" Kraler asks, joining them.

"I love you, man," Viper admits.

Kraler stares at him incredulously, afraid to grasp the underlying meaning in that confession.

"You ever thought of having sex with a guy?"

The three other members of the Council can't believe he actually posed him the question.

"Wow, Viper. You're starting to scare me now!"

"I'll be the female if you want. Any position you like."

"I ain't interested," he answers, amused.

"I'm tight. You'll love it."

Kral runs his hand over his mouth before giving a laugh. His threatening vampire warrior mask drops when he hangs out with these guys. He almost seems like a *normal* person. "I don't play for that team."

"I'll put on a dress and a wig."

"Stop it, Viper," he laughs. "Sorry to break it to you, but I'm a hundred percent into females."

Viper lets out a swear. He isn't only interested in women. He will actually bang anyone who comes near him as long as they look good enough for him to want to come inside them.

"We done?" Friz wants to know.

"Everything's ready. The bomb is finished. We can head off, bros."

"Do you want to go for a drink at *Byzance*?"

Kraler glances at his watch. Five hours. The sun should rise soon. "We don't have time for that. Let's go back home." The order is given. The five leaders of the Snakes clan leave the temple. Viper ogles Kraler as he walks away, taking long, feline strides. He definitely finds him sexually attractive tonight!

CHAPTER 23

Angel had a horrible week. Her exhaustion isn't even the problem at this point. There is a huge gap in her heart, something terribly painful that almost prevents her from breathing properly. She pines for him. She has no idea how such a thing is possible, but she misses him so much it hurts.

Kraler.

She is going to see Camilla tonight. She called her in the afternoon when it felt like there wasn't enough oxygen in the room, when the craving was so strong it almost tore her apart. Her anger has disappeared completely, as if by magic, and now it is a painful longing that consumes her.

Camilla arrives, disappointed. She has been going to *Byzance* every night but never caught sight of Slash. Angel tells her about the pain she has been feeling. "I need him," she concludes.

"I knew you'd be saying this. I have to say though, I didn't think you'd realize it so quickly. What are you planning to do?"

"I don't know."

"I do. Go and see him."

"He's never gonna want to talk to me."

"You don't know that."

Angel is dying to see him. She still can't understand how she changed her mind so fast but Camilla thinks it's because Kraler is imprinted in her. She loves him, that's all there is to it.

"Yes, I love him," Angel acknowledges.

"Do you have any way to reach him?"

"I have his number, but I can't call him."

"Why not?"

"I'd die if he hung up on me."

"We can go to *Byzance*?"

"I know where he lives."

"You do? I'm surprised he didn't blindfold you as he drove you back."

"I told you he didn't move as I left. I walked back home."

"Oh, that's right! So what are you waiting for?"

"I'm scared."

"I keep trying to stumble upon Slash but he's nowhere to be found, so please go and find Kraler before he mysteriously disappears as well."

"I need a shower."

"What a lame excuse!"

Angel's face breaks into a smile. An excuse to delay the moment when she'll have to go? Absolutely. She dreads the reaction he may have when he sees her there.

She shakes under the hot shower, wondering if going to see the vampire in the early evening really is a good idea. Camilla told her that the gang hasn't showed up at the club at all this past week. So, where is he? She imagines the intimidating giant depressing in his living room because of her. Impossible. Not him. So what is he doing? What if he was just... gone? All of them. She *has* to know. It's not like she can carry on like this much longer anyway. This has been the longest, most painful week ever. She is suffocating every second, it's inexplicable. Kraler can't possibly be the cause of her lack of oxygen yet it's the conclusion she drew.

While Angel is busy showering, Camilla's mind goes back to Slash. The untraceable Slash. The fact that none of the other vampires have been around lately reassures her a little. It means he's not hiding from her. They probably just have stuff to do. With more and more soldiers on their heels, they may need to hide. Well, she's probably just fantasizing but it helps her keep calm. Not being able to see the vampire is a real pain, although she doesn't feel it as strongly as what Angel decribed her.

"I'm ready," the latter says, walking into the living room. She is wearing tight jeans and a brown, cashmere sweater. She looks beautiful but on the inside, she is so scared she fears she might not find the right words when she finds herself facing the vampire. If she ever gets there.

"Well, hurry up then!"

"I don't know..."

"I do." Camilla gets up and walks towards her, taking her hands. "You miss him and you can't live without him anymore. If you want that smothering feeling to eat you up inside then you should stay here. If you don't, it's time you go and get things straight with him."

Angel takes a deep breath before letting go of her friend's hands. She grabs her purse and leaves the house without another word.

Don't rationalize. Don't think. Just keep walking.

She repeats those words in her head during the whole time it takes her to get to *Byzance*.

Don't rationalize. Don't think. Just keep walking.

Byzance stands in front of her with its door closed. Closed? How strange for a Friday night. She barely glances at the red sign informing people about the closure and carries on walking. She steps into a thirty-story building, takes a deep breath and gets into the elevator.

Don't rationalize. Don't think. Just keep walking.

She repeats the words over and over again as she presses "20" on the control panel. The elevator begins its ascent, stopping once in a while to load or unload people – both vampires and humans.

Twentieth floor.

Angel gets off with a lump in her throat. She remembers the way even though she was very upset the last time she was here. On the right. Straight on and then left. The door reads "19" in bold, black letters. Her heart thumps in her chest, pumping blood in her arteries at an incredible speed. She knocks on the door twice, so weakly a human ear would barely hear the sound.

"Come in. The door's open."

Kraler is here. She shudders at the sound of his voice. It seems as if an eternity has gone by since they last saw each other although it's only been a few days.

Come in. The door's open.

The words resonate in her. What if he was expecting someone? What if she was disturbing him? No time for questions. She walks into the apartment. A battle-gear wearing Kraler looks up at her as she closes the door. "Am I disturbing you?" Seeing him is so unsettling she can barely speak. The effect he has on her is unbelievable. She may feel weak and wobbly, she can definitely breathe normally now. Could it be true? That her breathing problem was the consequence of their separation.

"What do you want?" he asks, keeping on loading himself with weapons: a gun in his belt, a dagger, a blade in one of his pockets, grenades. He hides the collection under his long, black coat. One thing is sure: he definitely isn't depressing because of her.

"Can we talk for five minutes?"

"Two. I'll give you two," he declares, shooting a quick glance at her. "I have to hurry."

Two minutes. How can she say what she has to say in only two minutes? She hasn't prepared any monologue in advance! She's going to have to improvise, although she knows how bad an actress she is. How can she convince him that she is sincere? "I had enough time to think about all this and I'm not angry anymore."

"Good." His indifference doesn't really help her open up to him.

"Kraler, please, look at me."

He thrusts one last dagger into his coat before taking a step towards her. Their eyes lock. He is different. Very different. The only thing she notices is that all trace of humanity has left him.

"I don't have time now, Angel, so if you have something to tell me, I suggest you tell me now."

She tries to see past his dark gaze, which is probably nothing but a front.

"I miss you. I can't breathe when I'm not with you... I suffocate and it hurts like hell. I can't erase the horrible things I told you but I would like you to forgive me. I didn't mean them. I love you, Kral. I love you the way I've never loved anyone and... I never want to be separated from you again." She is quite proud of herself. She – sort of – managed to summarize the situation.

"Very well."

"What? That's it?"

"No. Of course not. That's not it." His black eyes seem to soften slightly, as if the ice inside of them was melting. She knew it was just a façade. "Wait for me here. Watch a film and we'll talk about it when I come back." He turns on the plasma TV and hands her the remote control. "Whatever you watch, there'll be a newsflash interrupting your program at some point."

"What are you going to do?" she worries, grabbing the remote.

"You'll find out at the same time everyone else does. I have to go, now."

He starts for the door and spins on his heels as she calls, "Be careful." He turns back and stops in front of her, softly trailing his hand across her face. His touch makes her hot.

"What you're going to see is the new Kraler. The new mission of the Snakes. Things are about to get serious. Here's the deal," he says, dropping his hand. "If you can't bear it, I suggest you leave before I come back here and I'll get it. But if you do that, please don't come back again to give me your speech about how you're not angry anymore and how you want to apologize. It'll be too late."

"What if I *can* bear it?"

"You wait for me here, but I don't want you to lecture me when I come back. I don't care about morals, I've taken my decision and it's final. Deal with it, or don't. Stay here, or leave. It's your call, but you can't change your mind once you've made your choice." She nods her head. "I'm going to be late." He

125

heads for the door and puts his hand on the doorknob before turning back. "I'm glad you're here. I hope I'll have a good surprise when I come back... darling." A smile, and he's out.

That wonderful smile was all Angel needed tonight. A feeling of warmth spreads through her chest. Just seeing him made her feel so much better. She is certain that everything will be alright now. Unless... Her eyes dart to the plasma screen. What is he going to do?

Kraler materializes in the manor, where the four other vampires are waiting for him.

"You're late, my Lord," Viper comments.

"Really? Again?" Slash laughs.

"Hell yeah! No, I'm just kidding. I had a wank before I came here."

"Good!" Kral puts in. "I don't want to distract you while we're on our mission."

"Don't worry about it, honey!" Viper replies with a wink.

"Alright, lovers!" Slash cuts off, laughing. "We have work to do!"

"We still have an hour," Friz informs them, glancing down at his watch.

"And I won't waste it talking about my absence of sexual intercourse with Viper!" Kral says, casting a sideways glance at his friend.

"Good, because I need to talk to you," Slash demands.

"What about?"

"Before you got here, I told the others about what happened with Camilla."

"Okay."

"I saw Stefan before coming here."

"They did close *Byzance* tonight, right?"

"Yes. He told me a beautiful female came by every night this week, hoping to find me there."

"Camilla?"

"She's not going to give up!" he sighs.

"What are you going to do?"

"Stay away from her. That female drives me nuts!"

"Stay away from the club for a while. She'll give up eventually."

"Otherwise I'll make sure she does," Viper decides.

"I don't think so. I'd rather do it myself," Slash objects.

"When? Before or after banging her?"

"You're spoiling for a fight, now!" Slash growls, slamming his fist against the wall.

"Enough!" Kraler snaps sharply. "No quarrels in the ranks! Where are the walkie-talkies?"

Friz leaves the room for a few seconds and comes back carrying the items, which he lays down on the table. Everyone grabs one – they will need them to keep in touch with one another throughout the night.

Less than an hour later, the five vampires materialize at the meeting point. It is dark outside and the sky is starless. They chose a forest about one and a half miles away from the military base. The fifty new vampire warriors who have just had the honor to join the Snakes are present and armed. Kraler gives a speech to motivate his troops – even though they don't really need it – and everybody goes off to their allocated spot around the base. The Beretta-wearing vampire warriors lurk in the shadows, waiting for the explosion to take action. They will have to shoot all the soldiers who will gather and try to help the survivors, but that's not all. Kraler has given the order to kill everyone else as well. Firemen and policemen. For now, he prefers not to hurt any civilian.

Friz, Dark and Slash cover Viper and Kraler who dressed up to go and set the bomb. It'll destroy everything within a radius of one thousand feet – the whole base. They need to place it in the center of the structure though, to make sure it will blow up all the surrounding buildings.

As Kraler fed off a civilian earlier, his capacities are at their maximum. He moves swiftly and without being seen, flanked by Viper, while the three others keep an eye on them from a distance. Each one of them has a sharpshooter's weapon.

Kraler leaps from building to building. His feline body can jump as high as seven feet. He is fast and undetectable to human eyes. No alarm goes off. He goes about like a real professional. Up on the roof of the central building, he sets the bomb. Next to him, Viper ogles him with hungry eyes. If the place was a bit more suitable, he'd try his luck again. Smiling, he watches Kral's big fingers work the bomb. "You ready, Viper? We're gonna take off at lightning speed."

"Whenever *you're* ready, my Lord. I'll follow you."

Kraler switches on the mechanism. They have exactly thirty seconds to move outside the one thousand feet perimeter. Jumping from roof to roof like two animals with sharp senses, they dash away from the dangerous area. Five seconds later, everything explodes in a deafening blow. It is a wonderful sight for the vampires and a feeling of pure ecstasy washes over Kraler.

The warriors come out of their hiding place, it is now time to attack.

Kraler bares his sharp teeth with intense pleasure. He doesn't want to miss a bit of the fight. Dagger in hand, he throws himself at the survivors.

CHAPTER 24

"We interrupt this program with breaking news..."

Angel's eyes dart from the bay window to the plasma TV.

"The military base has just blow up and vampires are attacking survivors by groups of ten. They are preventing the paramedics to access the burning buildings," the young reporter explains.

"My god... Kral," Angel sighs, covering her mouth with her hand.

Images of the disaster flash on the screen.

The fire.

Nothing but fire and debris where the military base used to be. It was one of the biggest in the state. One can see the vampires in the background, guns and swords in their hands.

Why?

Angel doesn't understand this totally uncalled for and cruel act of terrorism. It didn't seem like Kraler and his peers were really under threat. The soldiers never attacked them directly. David wanted them dead but she knew that the military men wouldn't be able to kill all the vampires. So, why?

Fire, debris, screams and tears are shown on the screen. The firemen arrive but the vampires stop them from approaching. If one of them steps too close, a vampire pounces at him.

Angel was far from imagining what Kraler was about to do. She understands why he wasn't as certain as her that she would still be there when he returned.

"The vampires are everywhere, attacking!" the journalist informs, terrified.

The firemen still trying to set up their fire hoses get killed by the vampires. She doesn't recognize any of Kral's friends but she can see that they all have a black snake tattooed on their left bicep. Their blueprint, it seems. The tattoo is displayed prominently – probably on purpose.

"We wanted peace," Kraler declares, grabbing the microphone from the journalist. He steps in front of the camera, his eyes dark with anger but also

jubilant. *"By trying to kill me and my peers, you only managed to kindle my wrath! It is only the beginning, gentlemen, if you decide to retaliate. Death will reign over this city if you send even one soldier in my district! There are fifty of us today but there could be many more tomorrow. Be wise, you motherfucking soldiers and leave us the fuck alone!"*

After his message, Kraler breaks the camera. The screen is filled with snow for a few seconds before another camera broadcasts the bloodshed. Angel swallows the lump in her throat. She doesn't know how long it will be before he comes back home but she needs to make up her mind. Quickly.

Kraler has changed, that's undeniable – she realized it when she saw his power-hungry eyes. She never would have thought he could do such an extreme thing. Will she be able to bear it?

But then again, she loves him so much she can barely breathe when she is away from him.

Tonight, she is breathing normally, she isn't gasping for air and she is certain that it is due to her presence in his apartment. If she leaves, if she goes away... she will suffocate to death.

Immersed in the bloodbath, the vampires exterminate the surviving soldiers but also firemen and policemen. Kraler and the members of the Council are loving it, especially Viper who not only drinks his victims' blood but rapes them beforehand.

How exhilarating for the leader of the vampire clan! All that blood. All that killing. All that power. The glory! He wants more and secretly hopes that the military will retaliate. They can't let them get away with him.

The Lord is back and kills people all throughout the night until the vampires decide to leave. Silence slowly replaces chaos. As the elevator takes him upwards, Kraler wonders if Angel is still there, if she stayed despite the massacre, if she is strong enough to support him and worthy of being at his side. He never would have asked himself these questions before but the recent changes in his life made him realize that he couldn't just choose any woman as his partner. She will need to have a wide pair of shoulders and unlimited tolerance. How can he ask that she accepts this when he just initiated a fight against human soldiers?

He sighs. She must have left – there is no other way.

He gets out of the elevator and starts for the door to his apartment when a smell tickles his nose. Flowers. A hint of spices.

How is it possible?

He opens the door and sees Angel, asleep on the couch. She didn't leave. A smile creeps across his lips as he slams the door shut, startling her.

"Kral," she says.

"I thought you'd be gone."

"I thought about it... but I couldn't," she admits, sitting up on the sofa. The next moment, she runs into his arms. He holds her tight, thinking that perhaps she isn't unworthy of him after all.

"Do I look good on TV?" he laughs quietly, pulling away from her.

"I don't understand why you did that."

"I've resumed my position as a war leader. It was time for me to pull myself together and guide my people."

"Your people? What the hell are you talking about?"

"I'm hungry. Follow me."

She trails him obediently towards the kitchen and sits on a stool, watching him cook steak.

"Are you hungry? Do you wanna eat anything?"

"No."

While he cooks, he tells her about his past, the title he inherited upon his father's death and then gave up on a while ago. He explains the reason of his choice, and those which led him to embrace his role again, to be a leader and get rid of the soldiers who make his life a living hell. The official reasons first, the ones the vampires all know: his digust, his boredom. And then the unofficial one, "You. Your rejection hurt me deeply and I could either react or die. I reacted, I got a grip on myself and took things in hand."

"Are you planning to exterminate all the humans?"

"No, I want peace. I said so on camera."

She doesn't believe a word he says. A man who truly wants peace would never act the way he did. He clearly wants war. "You perfectly know that the soldiers will chase you unrelentingly for what you did."

"That's what I'm hoping for. I want to fight, I want to make them bleed!"

"Kraler!" She was right not to believe him. All he longs for is blood and cruelty."

"I am a vampire, honey! What were your words, again? A monster. An animal."

"You're not a bad person."

"And you're here because...?" He eats the steak directly from the pan.

"I told you before you left. I feel like I'm suffocating when you're away."

"Okay." She was expecting more than a simple "okay". He seems so far away. Once he is done eating the almost raw meat, he storms back to the living

131

room. She follows him. He stands in front of the bay window and scans the horizon. No soldiers. No rebellion in sight. Angel walks up next to him, grabbing his arm and snuggling against his body as he stands motionless. The view makes her dizzy but she braces herself to stay close to him. "Kraler..." She tugs at his arm and he stares back at her, his eyes so distant it breaks her heart. She needs to feel him close. Now. "Make love to me."

He smiles. He is insanely handsome! "You're not the only one who's told me that lately."

An intense feeling of jealousy spikes through her. Other women? She swallows. *Did he do it?* "Who?" she asks timidly.

"Viper's been wanting me these past few days."

"Viper?" Her eyes widen. Viper, a homosexual? And she thought he was as straight as they come.

Kraler grins. She is dying to ask him if he granted his request but she doesn't dare ask.

He focuses on the night again, attentive to every sound, every movement. He's already forgotten the anecdote he just told her but she hasn't – she can't stop thinking about it and wondering whether he granted Viper's request or not. That would explain the distance he keeps between the two of them.

"Have you... well, you know."

He casts her a glance and bursts out laughing. Sometimes, it feels like the man she loves is back. At other times, it seems as if she doesn't even know the person she is facing.

"Who do you take me for? I don't play for that team!"

"Why does he find you so attractive all of a sudden?"

"Because I've pulled myself together. I'm finally pursuing my destiny."

"All that hatred, that blood, those deaths. I'm sure he must get hard just thinking about it!" she snarls, annoyed.

"Gets me hard too, so damn hard!"

The man she loves isn't here right now, that's for sure. He has no reaction as she pulls away from him. It hurts. His attitude towards her is very painful. She isn't quite sure what she was expecting tonight by coming here but certainly not *this*.

"It's so quiet out there." He turns his head at these words and notices the sadness on Angel's face. "Come here," he demands, holding out his arm towards her. Unable to protest, she steps forward and he draws her close. "I suck, tonight." He kisses the top of her head after that confession. Indeed, he could focus on her a bit more but he's waiting for the soldiers to retaliate – as they probably will. "I'm preoccupied," he admits, "I'll feel better when I know what's going to happen next."

"Is there even enough room in your life for me?"

He can sense the pain in her voice. Is there enough room for her? Yes. Of course there is. But he cannot forget the way she rejected him after saying those horrible things to him. That still sticks in his craw even though he would like to forget. He has to, if he wants to move on and have a life with her. He keeps her in his arms, in the silence, for a good hour until dawn. The first sunrays pour into the apartment across from him. He can feel the human girl's heart beating, her blood pulsing in her veins, but none of this catches his attention. He is focusing on something else: the soldiers marching in the streets, weapons in their hands.

"I knew it. This is going to be fun." Jubilating inside, he lets go of Angel and pulls his phone out of his pocket. "Check that out. They're looking for us."

"Where are the other vampires?"

"In a safe place. They'll never find anybody." He calls Viper to let him know about what is going on down in his street. Apparently, the same is happening in Viper's. "They go out during the day to be sure we won't attack."

"That's such an exciting situation. How much time left before the wonderful surprise?"

"I'll call the doc and ask him."

"Are you going to bed?"

"Yeah."

"Want some company?"

"Fuck off, Viper," he laughs.

"How long has it been since you fucked someone?"

"A few days."

"It's about time you let your hair down, my Lord."

"Forget it, dude. Keep in touch," he concludes before hanging up.

Angel overheard everything – Kraler is standing right next to her and Viper speaks pretty loud. A ridiculous feeling of jealousy overwhelms her suddenly. Kraler calls the geneticist straight away to find out how things are going. He had seen him several months ago to entrust him with a very well-paid task and had paid him a visit a few days ago with the Snakes to see how things were going – the night they had killed the young soldiers. The doctor answers promptly.

"How is everything going, Doc?"

"I found something."

"Tell me about it."

133

"A chemical agent that would inhibit the effect that the sun has on you, for a few hours."

"That sounds interesting. How long will it take before we can use it?"

"It's ready. I was going to call you today."

"I need 405 doses as soon as possible."

"I'll start right away."

"Let me know how things go, Doc. You will be greatly rewarded." He hangs up before dialing another number, Angel still at her side, listening to his every word. "Yassin, I have a request."

"It is a great joy to hear you, my Lord!"

"Time is short. I want the 350 remaining warriors to get tattooed as quickly as possible. They will be official members of the Snakes then."

"Your wish is my command."

"Let me know when that's done. And keep recruiting new people, Yassin, it's important."

"I've already started, my Lord."

"Perfect. I'll be eagerly waiting for your call." He hangs up the phone.

"My Lord? What the hell is that? What are you going to do, Kral?"

"I'm preparing a surprise for the soldiers."

"The 405 of you, attacking them?"

"If I'm not mistaken, they will only go out during the day to try and find us. They'll be hiding at night. If they want a war, they're going to have a war!"

"You're the one who declared it!" she objects.

"All I did was hit back and suggest that it should stop," he hisses.

"When I see how happy you are with the situation, I kind of have doubts about that!"

"Okay, I want this war. I'm going to fight in it, and win it."

"How?"

"Be patient, honey. I'm exhausted, I'm going to sleep. I have a long night ahead of me. Are you coming with me?"

She nods her head in agreement, although she feels overwhelmed by the whole thing and by the sudden hatred that seems to inspire Kraler. She follows him into his room. He takes his shirt off in front of her, telling her he is going to have a shower. It is the first time she sees the tattoo in his back.

A black snake.

Fascinating and terrifying at the same time.

She sits down on the bed, that bed she has already slept in before, but without him. She is burning with desire for him – the need and urge to give herself to him is consuming.

Kral comes back in the room with a towel around his waist. Angel's eyes wander on his handsome torso. She would like to caress it and run her lips across it. She misses him so much. He turns around to grab a pair of boxer shorts from the wardrobe, letting her admire his tattoo again.

"Your tattoo... is the sign of your membership to the Snakes clan, right?"

"Indeed."

She gets up and takes a step forward to brush her fingers against his skin. "It's beautiful." She keeps on caressing him, hoping he would spin around and take her in his arms before making passionate love to her – her body is ready to receive him. But he doesn't move and stands still, like a marble statue. A wonderfully beautiful and sexy statue, however immobile. Too immobile.

"Kral, make love to me," she demands.

"I don't have to fuck you everytime I see you."

His response leaves her speechless. He finally starts moving again as he puts on his boxer shorts, drops his towel on the floor and slips under the black silk sheets. "What are you going? Are you gonna bed down with me?"

She swallows the lump that just started forming in her throat. It is the last time he will hurt her like this. She makes that promise to herself! "No! I obviously made a mistake coming here. You've changed and I regret it. I don't want to see you anymore," she declares before leaving the room.

The door slams shut behind her a few seconds later. He sighs. Alright, he may have acted like an idiot towards her but come to think of it, he is convinced it was the right thing to do. He was unable to make a move on her – he didn't even feel like having sex with her. There is no more room for that female in his life now that he has declared war on the soldiers. He doesn't want her to stand in the way of his quest for power.

CHAPTER 25

A few days after the events, the military men lash out against Byzance. Without knocking or even waiting for an invitation, they burst into the club in force and wreck it, hoping that it will make the vampires come out of their hiding place but to no avail. The place is awfully deserted, nothing but a closed nightclub.

Kraler observes them from his apartment. The day has just started and he is standing in the shade. He smiles, baring his fangs which are thirsty for fresh blood.

Have fun, you motherfuckers. We'll destroy you soon enough.

He chuckles to himself before lowering the translucent steel blinds. From the outside, nobody could tell that the metallic blinds are down. The vampires are far from being stupid and from the outside, nobody can see where they live. The soldiers rummage through cellars and manholes. They are wide of the mark.

Another unpleasant day in Angel's life – as if it wasn't already full of those. She is not only unwell because of Kraler's absence but also abnormally tired. Camilla advised her to go see a doctor but Angel is so afraid of the diagnosis she can't even pluck up the courage to pick up her phone and make an appointment. The idea of suffering from a horrible disease scares her to death and eats her up inside.

Back at home, Angel gazes at her new table. It has been in her kitchen for only two days and it is much prettier than the previous one. Despite feeling awfully exhausted, she forces herself to cook. No more pizzas! Camilla must be getting tired of them! She goes for something simple: steaks and French fries. Her sister compliments her on the good smells as soon as she walks through the door. Angel, cooking! That's an uncommon event!

"I hope you're hungry."

"The smell makes my mouth water."

"Sit down then! It's ready."

The girls sit around the new table, christening it at the same time. The food is delicious and Angel devours her meal.

"Well, well! You must have been starving!" Camilla notes.

"I keep eating all the time, at the moment."

"Watch your weight."

"Give me one good reason to do so."

"You haven't heard from Kraler," Camilla understands.

"Why would I? He's too busy having fun with the soldiers."

"Did you hear about *Byzance* getting sacked, this morning?"

"Vaguely."

"It's going to open tonight. Apparently, they've redone everything today."

"Good for them."

"Tell me, Angel. Have you made an appointment with Doctor Alonso?"

"I forgot."

"Right. Or maybe you were just scared!"

"I might have cancer! I'm probably going to die! Excuse me for not being eager to find out!"

Camilla smiles. Her friend is ready to make up all sorts of excuse just because she can't be bothered to make a phone call. "Try this before panicking." She digs a small box out of her pocket and hands it to her.

Angel seizes it, expecting it to be some kind of anxiolytics that would help her make an appointment but... "A pregnancy test? What am I supposed to do with this?"

"You pee on it."

"Very funny!"

"If it's negative, I'll join you in your self-pitying," Camilla promises with a smile.

Angel puts the test down on the table and drinks her glass of water.

"Now," her friend demands.

The young girl sighs and grabs the small box. "I don't want a baby vampire!" she moans.

"Do it!"

She sighs again before complying.

"So, boss, what do you think about the renovations?" Stefan asks.

Kral scans the interior of *Byzance* with great interest. Stefan had the tables and chairs changed – they didn't really have a choice anyway, the soldiers

137

destroyed everything. He chose grey and red inox furniture and sober decorations.

"It's nice."

"Do you want something else to drink?"

"I'm waiting for the others."

"Fucking positive!" Angel cries out.

Camilla is waiting for her in the kitchen, a very sorry look on her face. "At least you know you don't have an incurable disease... It's pretty cool when you think about it."

The newly-pregnant girl keeps silent and stares at the damn test that just turned her whole life upside down. "I was planning to swing by *Byzance* tonight and look for Slash again. Are you going to come with me?"

"Why would I come with you?"

"Because you miss Kraler and you now have a good reason to see him."

"I'm going to humiliate myself once more!"

"Alright," she retorts, getting up from her chair, "I'll pop in before the curfew."

Since the base blew up, the military men established a curfew for all humans, forbidding anyone to go out in the streets after 8:30PM.

"Fine. I'll come with you."

At dusk, the Snakes meet up at *Byzance*. They are planning to relax and enjoy themselves tonight. Kraler needs to reenergize and so do the others before what they're about to do. After a glass of whisky, Viper goes off hunting females while the others stay and talk.

It isn't long before the tattooed boy sparks the interest of a pretty girl who finds him incredibly handsome despite his terrifying looks. He doesn't need privacy to make her reach seventh heaven and settles for a corner of the club, against a wall. He's not much of a romantic – his past prevents him from having normal sex. He treats them like pieces of meat – good meat, for sure – but meat nonetheless. He refuses kisses, eye contact and vaginal penetrations. He also does without the consent of the females he wants and couldn't care less about foreplay.

Once he is done with her, he goes back around the vampires table, feeling more relaxed. "I can smell fear coming from the soldiers," Viper laughs.

"I can't wait for them to find out about our little surprise," Dark jubilates.

138

"Be patient, my friends. Yassin is almost done getting our new warriors tattooed and the doctor has finished preparing three quarters of the doses we need. It's only a matter of days, now," Kraler replies.

Friz orders a second round of whiskies as a charming lady walks up to them. She has been ogling Kraler for a few minutes and he has definitely noticed her.

"Hi. I'm Candice."

"Kral. I'm here to have a good time with my pals."

"Need some help with that?"

"What do you have to offer?"

As a response, she places herself between his thighs and starts giving him a lap dance. Effective.

Very effective.

The city center is full of soldiers whilst the south district is devoid of them. Angel has told Camilla about Kraler's ambitions and his role in the recent events. She knew all that already though – she kind of figured it out when the program she was watching was suddenly interrupted with breaking news and Kral appeared on her screen, replacing the main character in the movie she was watching.

Angel has second thoughts upon walking into *Byzance* and hopes with all her might that he won't be there. It would just be easier that way.

"Forget about finding a table. What we're going to do is find them and join them at *their* table," Camilla decides.

Angel gives a sigh. She would have liked to sit around a table with her friend and have more time to prepare herself to confront Kraler. Again.

Camilla scans the room and immediately notices the change in the furniture. Angel feels like staring at the floor but she intinctively glances on her right, where she usually sees Kral. He is there. With the four others and a woman. She is overwhelmed with jealousy at the sight of this low-class girl giving him what looks like a rather erotic dance. A feeling of déjà-vu.

Kraler is having fun, smiling and laughing with the vampires, when his gaze is automatically drawn to the left. Angel is sitting a few feet away, staring at him.

Revenge.

He holds her gaze, his eyes darkening. He draws the female down on his lap and rests his head against her shoulder before kissing her in the neck. His right hand slips under the girl's tank top and grabs on of her breasts. With his other hand, he pulls down the strap of her top to reveal that same breast. He catches her erect nipple between his lips, still staring back at Angel who sits motionless as she watches. The sight of them is as pitiful as it is painful.

He decides to take things further, wanting her to quit coming back to him again and again. He runs his left hand beneath the girl's mini-skirt and sticks a finger inside of her, making sure Angel is still watching carefully. The girl whose name he has already forgotten arches her back and moans with pleasure as he keeps on stimulating her. His eyes are still riveted on Angel.

"Piece of shit," she whispers.

Despite the distance between them and the music, he hears her perfectly. She storms out of *Byzance* to cry. Camilla witnessed the whole scene and goes after her friend to comfort her.

"Fuck off!" Kraler orders sharply after taking his hand off the girl sitting on his lap.

She quickly leaves and he stares down at his fingers covered in her juices. Jumping up, he walks away from the table and towards the men's restroom to wash his hand with soap during several minutes.

Nothing.

He didn't feel anything while he was touching her, except for the desire to hurt Angel. From the way she bolted out of the club, he can tell it has worked pretty well. He shouldn't hear from her again, now. He can't deal with her constant changes of heart anymore. She keeps rejecting him and coming back a few days later. He can't deal with her human weaknesses, her need to overthink everything. Despite all this, he doesn't go back to the table after leaving the restoom. He goes outside, sees the girl and approaches them. "Camilla, go inside and sit at the counter. Nowhere else!" he decides.

As she refuses to move or listen to him, repeats the order in a more menacing tone. She obeys. He then focuses his attention on Angel, who is crying her eyes out, broken and fragile. All because of him and the stupid thing he did! He hates himself, all of a sudden. "I acted like a complete idiot," he utters, pulling her against him.

Unwilling to let him manipulate her at his will or forgive him, she pushes him away. "You're disgusting!" she shouts.

"I know."

"I never want to see you again!"

"So why are you even here? You keep saying you don't want to see me again but you keep on hanging round me for some reason."

"I don't hang round you!" she defends herself fiercely.

"Well, you're definitely here tonight."

"I'm pregnant, you idiot! That's all I wanted to tell you."

The Earth seems to have stopped moving all of a sudden. His ears inform him of a danger. A dormant danger. Pending. The soldiers. He draws Angel to him and hides her against his athletic body before bolting into the club. From there, he grabs her hand and hurries to his table. Camilla isn't there. He is surprised that she didn't try and talk to Slash. He slams his fist against the table and orders the vampires to follow him urgently. "The soldiers," he explains as they all dash off.

Passing the counter, he calls Camilla and Slash pulls her along as they go. They lock themselves inside Kraler's office. Thinking they are done for, Angel can already picture them getting killed and tears up at the thought.

Kraler activates one of the books in the bookshelf, revealing a passage behind it. They stumble into it and shut it behind them. Grabbing two of the torches hanging on the wall, they begin to climb down the stairs leading to what seems to be an underground passage. It's damp, dirty and cold. Still holding Angel's hand, Kraler leads the way, followed by Camilla, Slash, Friz, Dark and Viper. The group trundle along the tunnels for a few minutes. They go through a few armored code-locked doors and Angel notices that there are galleries in every direction. It is a real maze for anyone who isn't familiar with the place. After the heavily locked doors, Kraler activates a button hidden in the rock. A keyboard appears and the vampire enters another code, deactivating the deadly rays in front of them.

Not only a maze, the tunnels are also riddled with traps. Someone walking along them without paying enough attention would get killed without a doubt. After another couple of code-locked doors, they land in a library – inside a house, apparently.

The manor.

They all head for the computer set beneath the table. Kraler turns it on and the screen quickly displays the tunnels they just went through. "Everything's perfect," he observes. "Give me two minutes and I'll join you." He catches Angel's hand again and beckons to Camilla to follow them. Her eyes are set on Slash but he keeps avoiding her gaze. She obeys Kral and trails along after them. They walk up a stairwell and he leaves them there. "Second door on the left is my room. Go inside and don't move. I'll come back later," he instructs them sharply. Without another word, he bolts down the stairs.

CHAPTER 26

The girls walk in the indicated room. It is full of space and the bed in the middle of it is wonderfully large and appealing.

"Nothing happened the way I was hoping it would," Angel moans.

"I'm sorry." She suddenly starts gasping as if there was literally not enough air in the room. "Kraler?" Camilla calls. "Kraler? Kraler?"

He arrives soon enough, followed by the pack of vampires, and understands that Angel is suffocating. "Friz, call Lawson," he commands before hugging her tightly. "Calm down and breathe. Everything's okay."

Friz dashes off and the other vampires leave promptly afterwards as Angel manages to catch her breath. Slash doesn't lay eyes upon Camilla one single time but simply ignores her, as if she didn't even exist. Or as if she were transparent. Kraler lays Angel down on the bed and sits next to her, pulling her close again. Camilla watches them, alone in a corner.

"It's alright," he whispers in her ear, "I'm here." Incapable of explaining why she almost suffocated to death, he holds her against him as if to protect her from another danger. Not a word, just his strong arms around her as she slowly calms down.

Kraler leaves the room as Slater Lawson walks through the door, leaving Angel and Camilla alone with the doctor. The latter explains him what just happened and tells him that her friend is pregnant.

"Pregnant? And the father is one of the punks downstairs?" he laughs.

"Yes," Angel confirms.

"You're human," he says. It is an observation rather than a question.

"Yes."

"Did you get your pregnancy test in a drugstore?"

"Yes."

"We're going to verify it." He takes a sterile needle out of his small bag and pricks one of Angel's fingers, then spreading the droplet of her blood on what he calls a "pregnancy test for vampires". The red droplet turns blue. "You're pregnant alright."

Angel doesn't know whether she should feel relieved or even more confused now that her pregnancy has been confirmed.

"Miss, would you please ask the father to come upstairs, I'd like to have a word with the future parents," Lawson asks Camilla.

She gets out of the room to grant his request.

In the big room where they are all gathered, Kraler is arming himself. Camilla can't believe her eyes. "What the hell are you doing?" she asks in shock.

They all stare at her, trying to figure out who she's talking to.

"What now?" Kraler growls.

"Are you going to fight?"

"We just got attacked, right? Of course I'm going to retaliate!"

"What about Angel?"

"What about her?"

"The doctor wants to see you."

"Fine," he says. "Viper, call Yassin. I want all the Snakes ready to launch the attack in the south district as soon as possible."

"Will do."

Kraler climbs the stairs up to the room as Camilla shoots a look at Slash, thinking that it's about time.

"Did you want to see me, Lawson?" Kral asks as he steps into the room.

"So you're the future dad. Congratulations."

"What? Is that it?"

"No. I'd like to talk to you about your partner's pregnancy."

Partner? He arches an eyebrow. She refused that honor, but whatever. Doc doesn't need to know that.

"Since you're vampire and she's a human, the pregnancy will last seven months. A vampire develops faster than a human," he informs them before explaining that it only lasts five months for a female vampire pregnant with a male vampire's baby. He carries on by telling them about all the risks such a pregnancy might present for Angel. "That feeling of suffocation she's been having is directly linked to her psychological state. If she is feeling good and content, everything will go perfectly, but if something doesn't go right with your relationship, she might suffocate to death."

"She could die?" Kraler asks in shock.

144

The doctor nods. During such a high-risk pregnancy, it is vital for the female to have a good relationship with the father. If she stays away from him for too long or if their relationship deteriorates, she will get more and more fits. Kraler can't believe his ears. He is so upset he feels the need to sit down. "If I don't misunderstand you, I'll have to stay by her side at all times."

"No, Kraler. You won't need to be there permanently but you'll need to be around. And make sure you get along. No secrets, no quarrels. She will feel more and more needy as the pregnancy progresses. In short, she entirely depends on your attitude towards her."

"Fine. I got it. Leave us, now. One of my brothers will walk you back to the door."

Slater Lawson nods goodbye with a lift of the hand before leaving the room.

"I had no idea about all this," Kral utters.

"I need you. He was telling the truth."

"I understand it now."

"Stay near me."

"It's impossible. We just got attacked and my warriors are about to retaliate. I have to be there with them."

The fact that he considers that stupid – according to her – fight more important than her hurts so much. "Please. I need you."

"And I will be there, I promise." He pulls her against him and runs his hand up and down her back for a moment. "I'll be back. Promise me something." He cups her face with his hands and brushes her cheeks with his thumbs with infinite softness. "Don't die while I'm away." She smiles. "Just give me some time to take care of those flamers and I'll be back as quickly as I can."

She nods. He presses his lips against her, giving her a timid and way too short kiss to her liking.

"Call me if you really need me and I'll materialize here." He gets up and opens his wardrobe, instructing her to take one of his shirts to sleep as she waits for his return. He seems less distant than the last time they saw each other, but not close enough in the way she would like for him to be. "I have to go, now. Tell me you'll be okay."

"Come here, please." He gets closer and takes her hands in his before sitting down on the black silk sheets – the same he has in his bedroom at home.

"I'll be okay. I just need to feel you closer."

"We don't have time to talk, Angel. But be aware that I still love you," he admits, running his hand over her cheek. "Let's talk about it when I come back, okay?"

Her heart leaps in her chest at this revelation. He still loves her. That is more than she could hope for. "I love you too, Kraler. Be careful."

He gives a quick nod before laying one more kiss on her lips.

Camilla decides to approach Slash as Friz and Viper walk doctor Lawson back to the door. "Are you avoiding me?"

"No."

"I've been trying to see you for a while but you were never around."

"Really?"

"What's going on?"

"Nothing."

"Doesn't seem like nothing. You were nowhere to be found..."

"Don't know if you've noticed, but there's a war going on so I'm kinda busy at the moment."

"Okay. When can we talk, then?"

"I have nothing to say to you."

"I do."

She is so beautiful, so desirable. And all he can do is try and look indifferent when he is actually burning for her on the inside, the only female who has given him a hard-on in almost a century. And it is bound to happen again if she doesn't step back very soon. She's too close, only a few inches away from him.

"Everyone ready?" Kraler prompts as he storms back into the room.

An intense feeling of relief washes over Slash at the sight of his leader.

"Camilla, you'll spend the night here. I'll take you back home tomorrow when it's safe," Kral informs her.

"Are you going to leave her here all by herself?" She walks away from Slash and takes a step towards Kral.

He doesn't like her tone but reassures her nonetheless. "Everything will be fine."

"What was the human's problem, by the way?" Viper butts in.

Camilla shoots a glance at the vampire leader, waiting for his answer. Although she is dying to open her mouth, she won't say anything because she isn't directly involved in the issue. He's the one who should do the talking.

146

Kraler looks at each member of the Council, one after the other. "We'll talk about it some other time."

Camilla lets out a sigh. What a coward! He can't even tell them the truth. Can't even be there for Angel.

"Four door on your left. Get in there and go to sleep," Kraler commands, looking at her.

"You're disgusting! The way you behave with Angel is disgusting! And that stupid war on the soldiers only confirms to me that you are nothing! You were bored so you decided to turn our city upside down. You don't deserve her. I regret encouraging her to approach you earlier tonight." Her eyes then dart to Slash. "I'm not done with you. I'll find out what's happening." On that note, she bolts out of the room, not particularly interested in finding out the repercussions of her words.

"That girl's got some guts!" Viper notes.

"She better not talk to us like that again!" Kral snarls before letting out a swear word. "Let's get moving, gentlemen!"

"Let's go smash some faces!" Viper gloats.

CHAPTER 27

Camilla goes straight to Kraler's room to talk to Angel. Her friend is peering into the wardrobe.

"What did the doctor say to you?"

Angel picks a white T-shirt before closing the wardrobe doors. She then turns around to look at Camilla and explains her about the suffocating feeling, how the pregnancy will progress and how it all really depends on Kral's attitude towards her.

"And he still left despite all that!" Camilla yells, dumbfounded.

"It's alright, I promise. He'll come back."

"I reckon he could have stayed with you."

"He still loves me, Camilla," she beams, but her enthusiasm doesn't contaminate Camilla, unfortunately.

"I gave him a piece of my mind before he left."

"Excuse me?"

"And yet, it was before I knew about you! What I think of him now is even worse!"

"Camilla," Angel sighs.

"I so regret encouraging you to talk to him."

"And I'm glad you did. Everything will be okay, now. We'll talk when he comes back and we'll go through this together, I'm sure."

Camilla admires her optimistic vision of the situation. She would like to have the same but knowing Kraler, she doubts that it will be that simple.

"Were you able to talk to Slash?"

"He said everything was fine, the fucking liar!"

"Try and go somewhere alone with him if you want to make him talk. Maybe he doesn't like public demonstrations of affection."

"I won't leave before I've had a word with him." Angel lays Kraler's T-shirt on the bed as her friend goes on, "We're alone. Do you think we can check out the place?"

"Dauntless Camilla, wanting to check out a vampire house at night," Angel chuckles.

"Well, I think they'll probably be a while..."

"I think so, too."

Camilla beckons to her to follow her. They exit Kraler's room and climb down the stairs, landing in the big room where they were all getting ready a bit earlier. Angel immediately notices the laptop lying on the table – she opens it and the screen displays images broadcast by the surveillance cameras in the tunnels from *Byzance* to the manor. No alarm went off. Clicking on another open window, she discovers the plans of Kraler's apartment as well as the location of two alarms.

"*Byzance* is in the same street" Camilla notes.

"Kraler lives right across from it."

"I'll never tell anyone."

She clicks on the other open windows and Friz's and then Slash's apartment plans appear on the screen. "Can you write something down?" Angel asks.

"Ambaum Boulevard. Where's that?"

"We'll find out later."

"15B. Another apartment."

"You'll know where to find him if he tries to avoid you again." Angel brings back the plans of the tunnels into display before closing the laptop. They move on to the kitchen. It is bright and spacious. The furniture is in chrome inox. Beautiful. Camilla peers inside and asks her friend if she is hungry. "No."

They continue their exploration of the ground lever and make sure all the doors are locked and all the metallic blinds are down. Angel guesses that they must be translucid, in such a way that nobody would suspect anything from the inside.

"It's a real fortress," Camilla notices.

"Look at that," Angel demands. She has just found the armory. Daggers, swords and blades are hanging on the walls. A big crate full of grenades is lying on the floor. All kinds of weapons, small and big, are displayed on racks.

"They're not exactly choir boys," Camilla observes.

"I know Kraler has decided to resume his position as leader of the vampire clan – he's inherited the title from his father. He told me about his story and about his sudden decision. I know all about it, and I know I've hurt him a lot."

"Oh come on, Angel! If you consider what he's done to you, I think we can say you guys are even."

"Let's get out of here."

149

They go back upstairs because Angel doesn't wish to continue their exploration and Camilla wants to find Slash's room. She says she wants to borrow one of his shirts to sleep in, but Angel isn't stupid. They try every door until Camilla is sure they are in the right room – she recognizes the vampire's smell. She runs her hand across some of his clothes before opting for a stripy white shirt, then grabs a piece of paper from his desk and writes him a note.

Come find me when you're back. I'm burning for you. Camilla.

She leaves the note on his night table, hoping he will join her later.

"Where are you going to sleep?" Angel asks her.

"Don't worry, Kraler told me to go in one of the rooms."

"I'm going to wait for him."

"Call me if you don't feel well."

"I'll be fine." Angel goes back to Kraler's room as Camilla walks towards the one she will use for the night.

The vampire warriors started defending their territory from the invasion of the military men a few minutes before their Lord and the Council arrived. Bullets stream in from every direction. Both the vampires and the soldiers need to take cover to avoid getting hurt. The vampires' objective is to chase the intruders out of the south district. The latter eventually back out after a fierce battle – they are quite tenacious tonight, but so are the vampires.

There are casualties on both sides, a bit more on the human one. Just like cats, the warriors can see in the dark, which gives them an advantage over their enemies. By the time the clock strikes four, Kraler and his peers are in control. The leader instructs about fifty of his warriors to stay and patrol around the south district until dawn. He and the Council then leave the premises and quietly get back to the manor.

The decide to stay sheltered at home all day just in case the soldiers try to do something stupid in their neighborhood.

"Nobody allowed in Camilla's room!" Kraler commands firmly, his gaze darting from Viper to Slash.

"Don't worry, I have too much to lose," Slash assures him.

"Fine! I won't touch little Miss Angel!" Viper promises.

Kraler doesn't add anything and goes straight to his bedroom. He slowly pushes the door open and takes his clothes off in the dark as quietly as possible so as not to wake Angel. He'd promised they would talk but he isn't sure what to say. Everything's just fallen down on him, his decision to be leader again, his future paternity, the realities of her pregnancy. He's not certain he will know how to handle all that. He hasn't even had time to think about it. His mind is focused on the war they are running at the moment and there is room for nothing else.

Just as he is putting his clothes down on the armchair sitting in a corner of the room, the light switches on. "I didn't mean to wake you."

"I wasn't sleeping."

"I need a shower. I'll be right back." He disappears behind the door without another word.

As he is getting ready for bed, Slash finds Camilla's note on the night table. He lets out a swear word. She will never give up. Why is she even attracted to him? That scar in the middle of his face make him so ugly. Any sensible female would run away from him just because of that! Except for her.

Fucking female!

He cannot join her. No way. He knows what will happen if he does. He chooses to put on his sweatpants and unwind in the exercise room.

Kraler walks back into the room wearing close-fitting boxer shorts, causing Angel to gae hungrily at him. "How did it go?"

"We chased away the soldiers. A few warriors are still patrolling on the premises." He slips under the sheets and extends his arm so she can snuggle against his shoulder. "Are you okay?" He folds his arm over her once she is settled.

"I couldn't sleep. I was waiting for you."

"Do you want to talk?"

"I need to."

"I don't know what to tell you. I haven't had time to think about it. I feel like my head's about to explode."

She straightens up to look at him. With her right hand, she strokes his face. "Tell me what you want me to know."

"I don't care about that female back in the club and I'm sorry I acted like a complete idiot. I pushed her off me as soon as you left."

"We've already talked about that."

151

"You come to me, you tell me you want me again, and then you leave and slam the door behind you. It can't go on like this. I don't want you to leave again." He withdraws his arm and positions himself on top of her.

"I won't leave again. Ever."

A smile stretches a corner of his lips. "Everything just happened so suddenly. The soldiers, you coming back and now your pregnancy." He softly runs his hand across her face as she strokes his back, desiring him so much. "But I'll manage." He trails a finger around her lips. "I love you infinitely and you're going to have to promise me that you won't hurt me ever again. We have to communicate, Angel. I don't want there to be any problem between us."

"Agreed."

"So, I'm going to start... Your pregnancy..." he sighs, fumbling for words. The right words. "I've never thought about having a baby. But... I feel more than honored to be the father of your child." He presses his lips against her and gives her a long, staid kiss. "Would you accept to become my wife?"

"Yes."

He closes his eyes, relishing the moment. The moment she finally accepted ot be his forever and ever.

"I want you, Kral. I love you."

"We've done enough talking for now," he decides. "I want you, too." His mouth is on hers instantaneously as he lies down on top of her. There is nothing staid about this new kiss – he slips his tongue between her lips, exploring her mouth completely. Between two kisses, he whispers that he loves her. Angel doesn't remember ever feeling so happy.

His hands quickly explore her body before focusing on her breasts. He massages them for a moment, feeling more and more aroused. He licks her nipples sensually before trailing his tongue along her flat stomach. He takes his time with the woman he loves, driving her mad with desire, and finally sticking his tongue into the most intimate part of her anatomy. He savors her until he feels completely one with her... drunk on her juices.

It is only after her first orgasm of the night that he penetrates her with his manhood and begins to thrust in and out of her passionately.

CHAPTER 28

After working out and letting steam off for a few hours, Slash goes off to the kitchen and pours himself a glass of water. Now that he feels better, he can finally go to sleep without worrying about Camilla. Unfortunately for him, he stumbles upon the temptress on his way out.

"I was hoping I'd find you."

"I was just going to bed."

"What's happening, Slash? You're avoiding me and I don't understand why."

She looks hot in that shirt... Wait a minute! That's my shirt! Damn, she looks so hot in my shirt! "That's my shirt."

"I hope you don't mind. I wanted to borrow one of your clothes to sleep in."

"Sure."

She leans against the wall next to them and pulls him against her. There it goes again. All that working out for nothing – he feels desire washing over him like a tidal wave. The temperature in the room feels much hotter now that she is in it.

"I keep thinking about you," she whispers, wrapping her hands around his neck.

"So do I," he admits, unable to fight back the words.

"Don't hold back then, stop running away from me." She presses her lips against him and he gives him, kissing her back, abandoning himself in their embrace and sliding his tongue in her mouth feverishly. He pins her against the wall, pressing his hips against her, letting her feel his erection. His hands run up and down her back, over the fabric firstly but finding a way underneath very quickly. That dangerous embrace is making him hot... very, very hot. He cannot control himself anymore.

Without breaking the kiss, he begins to unbutton her shirt and then puts his right hand on her breast, his left hand still holding her tightly against him. Her skin is so soft and her cinnamon smell intoxicate him to the highest point. He

153

abandons her burning chest to slip his fingers in her, incapable of waiting any longer. He wants her. Now.

Camilla's body receive him with great pleasure. As soon as his fingers penetrate her, he feels her juices spreading all over his skin. He fingers her, his tongue still playing with hers. The young woman is consumed with pleasure and collapses against him as she climaxes. Nobody has ever made her come so hard. After pulling his fingers out of her, Slash takes his damp hand to the zipper of his jeans, impatient to penetrate her with his sex.

Just then, a voice rises behind them. "You've gotta be fucking kidding me!" Viper exclaims.

The trance in which the forbidden couple had been flops down instantly. Slash jerks away from Camilla. Viper sees his friend's fingers despite his trying to hide them. "Go back to your room," Viper instructs Camilla. His cold and threatening tone are more than enough to persuade her. She scuttles off without a word. "And you! Jesus fuck!" Viper shouts. "You can thank me, man!"

Slash turns to the sink to wash his hands, rubbing them with soap to try and erase the female's smell.

"To your room!" Viper orders as soon as he is done. The vampire obeys and his friend follows him upstairs. "What the fuck are you playing at?" he snarls, shutting the door behind them.

"I lost my mind."

"That's not the only thing you would have lost if you'd fucked her."

"Come on now! I didn't go that far!"

Viper takes a step toward the vampire and presses his hand against his crotch. "You're hard!"

"Thanks, I've noticed it too."

"Do you want to relieve yourself with me?" he proposes, pulling down his pants to show him his butt.

"Are you fucking crazy? First Kraler and now me?"

"Kral is banging his female. I heard them."

Slash shakes his head. The guy is everything but subtle. A lost case!

"Would you rather use your hand? Or one of mine?" he asks, showing him his.

"Enough with your bullshit!"

"As you wish. I just wanted to help, man. Don't go back in there. Do this for me, will you?"

"I'll try, but... yeah, I'll try."

"Have a good wank!"

Viper has his hand on the doorknob when Slash calls him back, feeling that if he lets him leave the room he won't resist the urge to join the girl who just made him lose control. "I want you to stay."

Viper smiles as he drops his hand to his side.

Alone in her room, Camilla hopes with all her might that Slash will come and join her. She doesn't understand why Viper interrupted them – it's not like they were doing anything bad. He must hate her because she used to go out with a soldier. That's the only justifiable explanation. What else could it be? Kraler has also been acting the same. Nobody wants her around Slash although it's obvious that he wants her. They're both grown-ups, so what's the matter?

She spends at least a half-hour mulling over the thought before finally concluding that if Slash refuses to tell her what's going on, she can just tell Angel to ask Kraler. That'll be the backup plan. But for now, she will continue to hassle Slash. She tiptoes out of her room, walking towards the vampire's with the light on in the corridor. Not very discreet but with all the statues and rugs on her way, she'd rather be careful and avoid falling down or breaking something. She quietly opens the door to Slash's bedroom and slips inside... She stops abruptly at the sight of the bed. He isn't alone in it. Viper is with him, his hand lying on his chest. She swallows hard before closing the door. So there, she has her explanation now: he is in a relationship with the vampire. Feeling deeply hurt, Camilla dashes back to her bedroom to cry her heart out.

Viper takes his arm off his friend, smiling. He had smelt the disgusting cinnamon smell as she was walking towards the room and had wanted to give her a good reason to leave Slash alone. Not for her own sake, but for the sake of the sleeping, snoring vampire lying next to him.

CHAPTER 29

It is three o'clock in the afternoon when Angel wakes up. She delicately lays her hand on the other side of the mattress, where Kraler is supposed to be, but she is alone in the big bed. She turns the light on, calling the name of his lover but no reply comes back. After having a shower and getting dressed with the same clothes she wore on the previous day, Angel leaves the room and joins the vampires in the kitchen.

"Hello," she mutters. She feels a bit uncomfortable, unaware of what they know or think. The way Kraler talked to her the previous day, in front of them, is still on her mind. They all reply politely. Viper smirks.

"I didn't want to wake you, you looked so peaceful," Kraler says.

She walks towards the bare-chested vampire. He only has sweatpants on and seeing him like this turns her on undeniably. She puts her hands on his shoulders before kissing one of them. He doesn't return the affectionate gesture. She watches him as he bites into his sandwich – ham, tomato and salad – after dipping it in his coffee. *Ew! He's got such weird taste!* Slash is devouring bowls of cereal, one after the other. Viper is dunking pizza in his coffee, Friz is having sausages and French fries and Dark is eating beans directly from the can.

"What do you want to eat?" Kral asks her between two bites.

"I don't really know. Don't you have anything... normal?"

"There's coffee. Slash, pour her a cup."

The vampire complies, asking her how she likes her coffee.

"With a lump of sugar, thanks."

He hands her the mug full of sweet coffee along with some buns, telling her that this kind of food is probably considered as "normal" in the human world. She smiles gratefully, sits down next to Kral and begins to eat. The latter is somewhat distant, pondering what he is going to do. Should he sort out this problem at the same time as his war against the soldiers or should he wait? That being said, his union with her isn't exactly a "problem." It's a very important thing to him.

"Where's Camilla?" Angel queries.

"Still sleeping," Viper answers.

Kraler puts his bowl in the sink after finishing his sandwich. "I'm gonna get dressed," he announces to the group.

Angel feels alone in the middle of the four other vampires. She eats without saying a word, avoiding their gaze. Friz and Dark pay no attention to her and quickly leave the kitchen. Slash gets himself another bowl of cereal whilst

Viper slurps down his coffee. "Things are better with Kral," he says, putting his bowl into the sink.

Angel looks up at the terrifying vampire. He's the scariest of all of them. "Did he say that to you?"

"He didn't say anything. I just heard you guys last night."

She feels herself blushing and doesn't dare to reply anything.

"Leave her alone, Viper," Slash intervenes.

"Alright my love," he retorts, blowing him a kiss.

Slash rolls his eyes, smiling. Once Viper is out of the room, he says, "He acts all mean and stuff but he's actually a very nice guy."

"Whatever you say." She's far from being convinced. Viper has a threatening air about him and that predatory smirk of his makes her incredibly uncomfortable.

"Kraler's had a smile on his face since he woke up."

"I don't know. I haven't really spent much time with him."

"Don't take it that way. It's not easy for him."

"I don't see why not."

"Kraler was a lone wolf. A pitiless, unscrupulous, unattached male, until the day he met you. It was hard for him to tell us about his wish to make you his partner. And you refused and left him. You hurt his ego and he thinks his leader image suffered from it. He loves you, I'm sure of that, but he's going to need you to prove him that you won't leave him this time. You're not planning on leaving, are you?"

"No, I'm not."

"I hope you're brave and tolerant enough. It wouldn't be fair to him if you left again."

"Hey, Angel," Camilla rasps as she steps into the kitchen, wearing the same clothes she had on the day before.

"Hey, Camilla."

Angel watches as Slash suddenly looks down. The atmosphere seems heavy, all of a sudden.

"Hi, Slash."

"Camilla. There is still some coffee and buns, help yourself. I'll leave you to it, girls." He puts his half-full bowl in the sink before scuttling off.

"He's avoiding me," Camilla sighs, pouring some coffee in a cup.

"Did you talk to him?"

"We did a bit more than that..." she replies before telling Angel about the short moment of intimacy they shared.

"Wow!"

"It won't happen again."

"Why not?"

"He's already with somebody."

Angel gives her an incredulous look. She's never heard or seen anything that would lead to that conclusion.

"Viper interrupted us. Later when I wanted to join Slash in his room, he wasn't alone in his bed, and from what I could see, he was naked."

"Who?"

"Viper."

Angel lets out a giggle, but as her friend stares back at her with a desperate look on her face, she understands that it isn't a joke. "Oh come on! Viper and Slash? Nonsense!" Then she remembers what Kraler told her about Viper trying to seduce him. Maybe the vampire really is gay.

"Are you ready?" Kral calls, stepping into the kitchen. "I'll take you back home."

Angel lays her eyes upon the sexy vampire, now wearing black jeans and a black turtleneck top. The guy really has a knack for turning her on.

"Yeah, alright. I'm not even hungry," Camilla replies.

"What about the soldiers? Are they not out there?" Angel worries.

"They are."

"What are you going to do?"

"I'll drive you back to *Byzance*. A taxi will be waiting for you there."

"How about you? What are you planning to do?"

"I have important stuff to take care of."

"I hope I'm part of it." She would like for him to agree and ot tell her about his decision to announce their future union to the other vampires, but...

"I'm dealing with one thing after another. The soldiers first. It won't take more than a few days."

"I need you, Kral."

"And I will be there, as promised? But I want to run this war without you. It isn't the right place for a female."

She doesn't know how to take it. In any case, she agrees that it isn't safe for her to stay around him during the war but if she's going to be his partner, she would rather go through it all with him. Even through the war.

"Come on, females! I got stuff to do!"

The girls trail after him as he starts for the big main room where all the other vapires are waiting.

"I'm going to drive the girls back to the club. I need one of you guys."

"I'll go," Viper replies, glancing at Slash, who obviously would like to go with them.

Kraler beckons to the girls and they move along, followed by Viper. They go through the same tunnels as the previous day, slipping into the passage behind the bookshelves. Kraler grabs Angel's hand, holding a torch in his other hand. The lights are only there for the humans, as they can see perfectly in the dark. Leading the way, Kral often needs to let go of Angel's hand in order to type in the codes which are needed to open the doors or deactivate the traps. They progress silently through the tunnels until the vampire leader pushes the door to his office in *Byzance*. Viper moves ahead of them and makes sure it is safe before letting them in.

"Kral," Angel whispers, holding him by the hand.

The vampire turns around and understands that she would like a word with him. "You guys go ahead, we'll join you," he decides.

Viper and Camilla get out of the office. Kraler stands next to Angel, waiting to hear what she has to say.

"I want to be with you."

"I have things to do. It's important."

"You're not listening! I want to be with you!" she gasps, losing her cool as she struggles to express the burning feeling inside of her.

"I'm here," he replies, putting his hands on her shoulders. "The thing is, I have obligations."

"How long will you be?"

"I don't know."

"I won't see you in a while, then," she assumes without trying to hide her sorrow.

"Do you know what we're going to do?" She shakes her head. "You're going to go home and grab your things. Then you can come back to mine." He drops his hands from her shoulders and digs one into his pocket, pulling one a set of keys. "These are the keys to my place," he says, handing them to her.

She takes them, smiling. She won't feel so lonely without him if she stays at his place.

"I'll do what I have to do and then I'll join you there. Alright?"

"Yes." She slips the keys into her pocket before putting her hands on his hips and moving closer to him. He draws her against him immediately. "I'm going to miss you."

"Don't worry, I'll make you forget about that as soon as I'm back." After that kind-of promise, he presses his lips against hers and kisses her passionately, their tongues playing with each other. Angel steps back and leans against the desk, drawing him with her. She sits down on it, legs spread. He fills the space between them and presses his lower body against hers as hard as he can. Her whole body is begging for him.

"You're making me hot," he breathes, kissing her throat.

"I can give you even more."

"I don't doubt that. But not now." Matching words and actions, he straightens up and breaks the embrace.

"I know. You have obligations."

"And the sooner you let me go, the sooner I'll be back."

She straightens up as well and nods, missing him already. He holds out his hand and she grabs it, pulling him against her chest for one final hug.

Viper has been pacing the spacious nightclub for five minutes while Camilla is sitting down at the bar.

"I'm sure they're going at it again!" he laughs.

"Excuse me?" Camilla asks in shock.

Chuckling, Viper walks closer. For the first time, he doesn't look threatening and she doesn't fear him. Actually, he's quite handsome when he smiles.

"Kraler. He banged his female during half the night. They're probably doing it now, if you want to know what I think."

"You're so rude!"

He might be handsome and less threatening, but why does he have to be so rude?

"How 'bout you, honey? How's the sex with mister soldier?"

"I'm not with him anymore."

"Really?" She doesn't reply, but he sure isn't going to leave it at that. "Oh, right! You're totally into Slash, now. What an amazing change!"

Slash! She perfectly remembers the position he was in last night... with Viper at his side.

"He's not interested," Viper tells her.

160

"Because he's with you?"

He laughs out loud, baring his teeth. "I know you saw us. I detected your smell near the room." As he doesn't deny it, she doesn't badger him any further. It only confirms what she already knew and it hurts so much. "You don't want me as your enemy so you better stay away from my man, or I'll bite!"

Although he isn't very menacing, she feels herself shivering in terror. He could kill her so easily. Anyway, Slash is in a relationship with the guy so she had better not declare war to him. There is no more hope for a future with the man she loves.

Kraler and Angel enter the room.

"Finally!" Viper sighs. "Haven't you had enough last night? Jesus! You're a fucking sex machine!"

"Did you hear us last night?" Kraler asks.

"Teach your female to shut it up if you don't want us to hear her moan! Or control your sex drive for God's sake!"

Kral doesn't reply anything, which surprises Angel. Letting him speak to him that way without telling him off – that's quite strange, coming from Kraler.

"So shall we put her in a taxi, already?" Viper teases.

"Why, are you impatient?" Kral laughs, arching an eyebrow.

"Yeah baby. I want to feel your cock inside of me!"

Viper and Kral burst out laughing. Regaining his composure, he turns towards Angel, "Call me if there's anything wrong."

"Are you sure I can leave you with that... lunatic?"

He smiles.

"The taxi is waiting outside. Go, now."

She smiles too, feeling desire burn her skin. She'll have to wait for it, though. Now isn't the time to think about melting at his touch. She gets closer to him and kisses him. He hugs her tight and slides his tongue into her mouth.

"Come on, now! Here they again!" Viper says, sighing. He glances at Camilla.

"What?"

"Are you interested in a hot sex encounter?"

"With you? No;"

"Alright, Viper!" Kral puts in. "I'll let my female go."

"It's about time. I'm gonna get real hard if you keep on making out like that."

"I'll see you later," Kral promises Angel, ignoring his friend.

The girls quickly get out of Byzance, using the back door, and climb into the taxi waiting for them.

"Everything alright with your girl?" Viper queries.

"Everything's getting complicated."

"Wanna talk about it, dude?"

"She's pregnant."

"Shit! That's what happens when you can't control yourself!"

"It isn't funny!"

"I see. What are you going to do?"

"I'm going to make her my official partner."

"Seems pretty logical. Do you love her, though? Don't trouble yourself with a chick you don't give a damn about. I can take care of this, if you want."

"Don't touch her, Viper. Whoever lays his dirty paws on my female will suffer dire consequences. When I'm done with the guy, he won't even be able to walk again or even get a hard-on."

Viper puts his hand on the giant's shoulder, smiling. "Wow, that bad, huh?" he laughs.

Kraler gives a nod.

"Hey, I meant to tell you something."

"What?"

"Camilla was trying to seduce Slash again last night. I had to intervene..."

"Tell me he didn't—"

"No. However, I spent the night with him to make sure it wouldn't happen again."

Kraler gives him an incredulous look. Viper and Slash together, in the same bed? He won't ask the question though – it's none of his business.

"It was the right thing to do – Camilla tried her luck later again."

"What do you mean?"

"She slipped into his room in the middle of the night but she quickly went back to her room."

"Why?"

"Slash and I were in bed together, naked. I had my arm over his chest."

Wow! He wonders if it was planned or if it just happened. Did it even happen for real? If he was as direct and rude as Viper, he'd ask him.

"We talked about it when you were with your female. I told her to stay away from my man."

"What the hell are you saying, then? That Camilla won't be an issue anymore or that you're fucking Slash?"

162

"She won't be a problem anymore, boss! As for the rest, I thrust my cock in whoever I like!" he says, laughing.

"Damn right."

CHAPTER 30

Camilla and Angel ask the taxi driver to take them back to Angel's house, where she quickly fills a bag with her clothes and toiletries. She doesn't know how long Kraler will be but she can't wait to go back to his.

"I have a voice mail," Camilla says surprised as she turns on her phone.

"Was your phone off all this time?"

"Yeah."

She plays the message. *"I miss you Camilla. I need to see you. Please come and see me."*

"It's from David. He wants to see me."

"Are you gonna go?" Angel queries on her way to the bathroom.

"Dunno," Camilla replies, following her. "I talked to Viper when you were locked in the office with Kraler."

"He must have been horrible to you, I'm sorry."

"Not really, actually. He's kind of a nice guy once you get past the 'rude bastard act'. He told me to stay away from his man."

Angel drops a – plastic, thank God – bottle of shower gel in shock.

"He's in a relationship with Slash," Camilla adds.

"Fuck! I'm sorry. I never would have imagined."

"So... I might go and pay a visit to David, see what he wants."

"Everything's ready," Kraler announces to the Council after hanging up the phone.

"So who's going to fetch them?" Friz queries.

"We'll all go together at 10PM, at his lab. We'll bring them back to the temple afterwards."

"When are we going to launch the surprise-attack?" Dark asks enthusiastically.

"The sooner the better. I want to end this as quickly as possible."

"A particular reason for that?" wonders Slash, who seems less present than usual.

"I'm going to organize a union-ceremony. Angel will become my official partner – or wife."

"You guys are getting along again, that's good."

"While we're at it, I might as well let you guys know that she is pregnant with my child, but that doesn't have to do with the fact that I want to marry her."

The members of the Council exchange surprised glances. Viper, who already knew, folds his arms across his chest and waits for the surprise effect to fade off.

"Anyways, we'll make a decision about the attack tonight, at the temple," Kral declares.

"Is Yassin done inking the new warriors?" Viper asks.

"We'll see that tonight. Tell him we're on our way."

Viper nods in agreement.

Camilla and Angel leave the house but go different ways after a few minutes. Angel heads for the south district whilst Camilla stays in the city center. She knocks on David's door without great conviction. He isn't sure he will be home although it's a Saturday, but the door promptly swings open and a clean-looking and smiling David appears behind it.

"I'm glad you came."

She walks into the apartment and notices how tidy it is compared to the last time she came. He was a complete slob back then. "Why did you want to see me?"

"For two reasons. The first one is the most important: I miss you."

She already knows – he told her in his voicemail. The thing is, she has no idea how to react. It feels weird to be here with him now that he's his old self again, but she isn't going to throw herself into his arms again just because Slash already has someone... that would be insane.

"I'm sorry I failed our relationship when you're the most important person to me."

"You're not the only one who failed."

"Have you... met someone else?"

Telling him about the vampire would be a huge mistake, so she keeps quiet, leaving him to interpret her silence.

"Do you want something to drink? I have soda, Orangina..."

"Soda will be fine."

He starts for the kitchen as she sits down on the couch, and comes back a few seconds later holding two glasses of soda. "I still love you, Camilla," he confesses, stroking her hand.

She feels like she is suffocating but it isn't because she feels the same way. It is because she has no idea how to get herself out of this tricky situation. "That's not what I'm here for," she replies, taking her hand away.

"You didn't know why you were coming but you still came."

"Maybe I shouldn't have. I don't want... to get back together with you." She takes a sip of her soda, waiting for his reaction.

His face is unreadable.

Back at Kraler's, Angel settles down. She has no clue what time he will be back but she hopes she won't have to wait for too long. The sun shines through the bay windows and the streets seem empty. Ever since the soldiers started patrolling during the day, humans have been scarce. It isn't long before her phone starts ringing and she picks up as she reads "Kraler" on the screen.

"Are you at my place?"

"Yes."

"Will you please lower the steel blinds?"

She pushes the button and the metallic blinds start descending. She can still see outside but the sunrays are completely absorbed. Translucid steel. Very clever.

"Done." The ringing tone starts beeping in response. He's already hung up. She puts the phone back in the pocket of her jeans, not knowing what to think, when Kral bursts into the apartment.

"I'm free till 9:30," he announces happily.

She glances down at her watch – it is 6PM. She is glad about being able to spend the next few hours in his company. She's been waiting for so long... wanting him all for herself. She gets closer to him as he takes off his long black coat, throwing him on the sofa before pulling her in his arms.

"My love," he breathes.

"Everything went according to plan?"

"Yes." He untightens his grip to look at her in the eyes. "I told my friends I was planning to marry you very soon."

She smiles in wonder – she wasn't sure he would do it and thought it would take weeks.

"I also told them you were pregnant with my child."

166

"How did they react?"

"Once the surprise effect was over, you mean? Everything's fine."

"When will I be able to call you my... my what, exactly?"

"We can just use the word 'husband'."

"Okay. So when will I be able to call you my husband?"

"I can answer that question when we've decided exactly what we're going to do."

"You mean tonight?"

"Yes."

"So we have three and a half hours... How could we spend that time?" She walks away from him and takes a few steps in the room.

"I have an idea," he says, taking off his black sweater and tank top all at once.

She admires his chiseled torso, his stone-hard pectoral muscles. He is the definition of the word "perfection". Sexy and frightening at the same time as he bares his teeth. She is already turned on and he isn't even naked yet.

"What's your idea?"

He unbuckles his belt and then unbuttons his jeans before pulling the zipper down. If he's trying to drive her crazy, then he's very good at it – her panties are all wet.

"I could make love to you during three hours and then feed."

Feed? On her blood? She doesn't know if she feels ready to give that to him yet. The whole idea still scares her. As if aware of her worries, he adds that he was talking about a juicy steak.

"I like the sound of your plan."

"Good. Then let's not waste any more time."

He kicks off his jeans and strides towards her, pulling her into his bedroom undressing her and lying down next to her underneath the black silk sheets. He strokes her for a bit and then catches her lips to kiss her feverishly. Their tongues caress each other as his erected shaft rubs against Angel's pelvis. She doesn't know how much longer she can wait until he penetrates her. With his right hand, he strokes her perky breasts, her nipples hardening with desire for him and then her stomach. He plays with the sexy ball of her belly-button piercing – he's always found it incredibly arousing. He abandons her feverish mouth and begins to lick her abs and the area around the piercing. He then penetrates her with his tongue, making her moan. He explores every part of her crotch, giving her intense pleasure which she expresses aloud. After making her come, he straightens up to kiss her, driving his manhood into her at the same time. A sensual thrusting begins and they both reach orgasm. After unloading inside of her, he pulls her into his arms.

"You're the first woman I've ever done this to."

She sits up and turns her face to look at him. His forehead is covered in sweat – he turns her on so much. All the more so as she knows he will make her come again before leaving.

"You've had sex with other women, though."

"I've never done to them what I do to you. I've never kissed them. Never licked them anywhere. Never caressed them or allowed to caress me. As for my sex, none of them has ever touched it."

This confession gives her such a sense of privilege she feels like taking advantage of it. "You mean, nobody's ever done this to you?" she asks before French-kissing him passionately.

"Never."

She kisses him in the neck before running her tongue across his chest, down to his nipples. "How about this?" She pinches them one after the other as he scrape his hand through her hair, moaning.

"Never."

"And this?" She licks his stomach and starts stroking his long and hard sex with her right hand.

"Nobody," he moans.

"What about this?" She replaces her hand with her lips and then her tongue, wrapping her mouth around his cock. He gasps with pleasure as she starts giving him head hastily.

"Never." He enjoys the moment and the burning desire inside of him, wanting her badly. Again. And her blood, too. He can actually smell her delicious flower scent but this time, he won't lose control. There is no way he is ever going to hurt her again. After coming, he draws her against him, impaling her on his erected penis, letting her decide on the rhythm. He relishes all the pleasure she gives him. He is euphoric and sweaty when she is done with him. It is usually her, who feels to insanely good afterwards to the point where she can't even move. It's his turn, this time. And she loves making him feel that way. The feeling of control. He is hers as much as she is his.

"I love you," he pants, "More than my own life."

"I love you so much, Kral."

"What you've done to me has made me fucking hungry but I can't feel my muscles anymore. Can't move."

"Neither can I," she replies, licking his throat and jawline.

"Do you think I can bite hard enough to cut through your skin?"

"I think it would probably hurt like hell."

"Oh! But you're a giant!" she laughs, exhilared. She is over the moon. It makes Kraler very happy to see that the sadness in her eyes is gone. Even if he is sometimes away or distant, he is here right now and we won't abandon her when she needs him ever again.

"Do you feel like drinking my blood?" he queries.

"I want to become your official partner, according to the customs of your people."

He is surprised. He had told her about his desire... that burning desire in his veins. He never thought she would accept though, considering the reaction she had when he first talked to her about it. "I shall give you my blood and drink yours while we make love after our union."

"It would be an honor." She kisses his lips before getting up from the bed promptly. For once, she isn't the one who feels like she was just crushed under a steamroller. He is.

David takes a sip of his soda and apologizes to Camilla, "Since the first thing I had to tell you is an epic fail, let's move on to the second one." She casts him a puzzled look, wondering what he is going to come up with. "Tomorrow, the soldiers will evacuate all the civilians from the south district of Seattle. You are not to go there again."

"Why are they evacuating people?"

"You're aware of what's been going on these past few days."

"I saw the news like everybody else. You're attacking the vampires."

"The Snakes started it."

"So? Why the need to evacuate? I don't understand."

"It's a military secret."

"Well you started talking about it David, so carry on. Otherwise you shouldn't have said anything at all."

"The evacuation will start from the crack of dawn so tell your friend not to hang around the corner."

"Will I be allowed to go there after the evacuation?"

"No. They're going to blow the place up... all the vampires are going to die."

Her eyes widen in shock. The soldiers want to blow up the south district! That's completely insane! "That's a pretty extreme solution!"

"The state will finance its reconstruction and in the meantime, the homeless humans will be allocated council housing. Rest assured that there aren't many of them, though. The south district is plagued by vampires."

"I won't hang around there tomorrow. And I'll let Angel know."

"I hope she's still keeping a distance from the vampire, isn't she?"

"Yes," she lies convincingly.

"Are you hungry?" Kral asks Angel, taking a steak out of the fridge.

"Just a little."

"Do you want a piece of rare meat?"

"No. I could do with a yoghurt."

"Is that how you intend to feed my offspring? With a yoghurt? No way. Have a steak." She watches him put two pieces of raw meat on the gril. He's only wearing boxer shorts and looks amazingly attractive. She put one of his shirts even though she brought her own clothes. He starts eating his steak whilst she wait for it to cook a bit longer. "I'm going to get ready," he says.

"Don't run away so fast."

"What?"

She sits on the table and spreads her legs, beckoning to him to come closer. "Don't tell me you were expecting me to watch you hang around in those shorts and not get turned on?"

"Are you turned on, then?"

"Come here, I'll show you how turned on I am."

He stands between her legs, leaning forward to kiss her throat before fulfilling her desires. "I really need to go," he breathes against her throat.

"I know."

After one last kiss, he leaves her on the table, heads for the bathroom and has a hot shower. The young woman does the washing-up in the meantime and cleans the hot plates.

"Angel?" Kraler calls with his phone in his hand. "Camilla just called me."

"Did she want to talk to me?"

"Actually, I wanted to talk to her." She is surprised; why would her friend want to talk to her boyfriend? "The program just changed, my love. Go get ready, you're coming with me."

"Why? What's happening?"

"I'll tell you later."

Obediently, she goes to have a shower while Kral calls Viper.

"Listen to me carefully. Go and get Camilla and then take her back to the manor."

"What the hell?"

"The soldiers also have a surprise for us."

"Yay! Consider it done."

"She's waiting for you."

CHAPTER 31

A black Lamborghini parks in front of Camilla's building. Coming out of it, Viper climbs up the stairs to her apartment and knocks on her door. She opens it.

"I was waiting for you," she says. "Come on in."

He smiles and walks in, taking in the interior as she closes up her bag. The apartment is small, the furniture is all over the place but it is also quite stylish. If he didn't know a woman lived here, he definitely would have guessed it.

"I gathered a few things, as instructed by Kraler."

"What's going on, anyway?"

"He hasn't told you?"

"Apparently, the soldiers have a surprise for us."

"And a pretty big one at that."

"How come you know what's happening, and I don't?"

She picks up her bag and walks out of the apartment, followed by Viper. Locking up the door, she answers, "I'll tell you on the way."

"I parked the car right in front of the building."

She trails after him in the street, puts her bag in the trunk of the Lamborghini and sits down in the passenger seat. He starts the engine and the monster of a car roars as it drives away into the night.

"I heard that the soldiers were up to no good."

"What do you mean?"

"They want to evacuate people from the south district of Seattre tomorrow and then blow up the whole area."

"Wow! How do you know?"

"My ex told me."

"Yeah, your ex. The soldier. Why would he have told you that?"

"He doesn't want me hanging around there tomorrow."

"The guy even gives you orders?" he jibes, "Too bad for him, but you'll definitely be there."

She's aware of that – Kraler told her she would stay in the manor until Sunday. The manor obviously has to be somewhere in the south district.

Kraler's grey Corvette pulls up in the manor driveway after driving through the electric gate. He gets out of the car, grabs Angel's bag from the back seat and takes her hand. They start walking through the dark, towards the entrance door. Friz, Dark and Slash are in the big room they use as a meeting room when they walk in.

"Viper isn't here, yet," the leader notes.

"He stormed out ten minutes ago," Slash explains. "Apparently, you know why."

"I'm going to tell you everything."

He goes upstairs with Angel and puts her bag in his room before turning towards her. "You already know the whole story. You can either stay here or come downstairs with me and listen to our attack strategy if you wish to."

"I want to stay with you."

He squeezes her hand, stroking her palm with his thumb. Taking her fingers to his lips, he kisses them softly. The next moment, they join the others back in the living room. Kraler sits at the far end of the table – on the leader seat – with Angel by his side. "Friz, call the doc and tell him we'll be slightly late," he decides.

The vampire executes the order and makes the phone call.

"Here we ware!" Viper beams, walking into the room with Camilla behind him.

The young lady drops her bag on the floor as Slash wonders what is going on. What is the temptress doing here?

"Camilla had the great idea to pay a visit to her friend the soldier, today," Kral begins.

Friend? Slash perfectly knows that he is her boyfriend. Well, at least he believes so since nobody told him otherwise.

"He told her what those bastards are about to do tomorrow morning."

Kraler watches Camilla as she moves closer to the table and starts speaking, telling them about the soldiers evacuating all the human civilians from the south district as soon as the sun comes up. Then, she explains that they will simply set a bomb in the buildings, destroying the neighborhood and the vampires completely.

"Why did he tell you such an enormous secret?" Slash queries, thinking how stupid the guy must be.

"Because he doesn't want me hanging around the area tomorrow."

"Doesn't he know that you associate with us?"

"No."

"He does know that your friend is with our leader, though."

"He thinks they've fallen out. I didn't deny it."

"You lied to your boyfriend, then. And you're betraying him right now."

"He isn't my boyfriend anyore, I broke up with him a while ago. And I'm not betraying him, I'm saving your asses."

He nods, saying nothing. Camilla is single. It would have been so much easier if she was in a relationship with somebody.

"So, what's the plan?" Dark wants to know.

"Let's bring forward our surprise attack," Kral decrees. "We'll attack as soon as they show up in the morning to evacuate the humans."

"I can't wait," Viper rejoices.

"Now let's go and collect our syringes. We'll take them to the temple tomorrow and give orders," Kral explains. "Tomorrow's gonna be a banging day!"

The vampires exchange ideas and thoughts. Four hundred vampire warriors will attack the military men. The latter will probably be fewer, unsuspecting of the vampires' action plan. Moreover, there are very few humans living in the so-called "plagued" district. Logically, the troops will be in the minority and all they will have to do is take them by surprise. And what a surprise!

"The next few days will be long, my friends; we will have many things to deal will and I won't have much time to dedicate to my female. I want to marry her at the temple. Tonight." All eyes dart to Kraler. Even Angel didn't know about his intentions. "How does that sound?"

Gazing at her, he anxiously waits for her answer. After all, she's already said "no" once. She could do it again. And it would be even worse for him if she did so in front of the Council.

"Yes. That's all I want."

A smile stretches his lips. He instructs everyone to get ready before the departure. Moving closer to Angel whilst the others begin to arm themselves, he grabs her hand tenderly, lifts it up to his mouth and kisses it. "You're going to come with us, but you must make a promise to me."

"Anything you want."

"Follow my orders word for word."

She nods in agreement as he says the same to Camilla, who accepts the deal as well.

174

The group leaves the manor and divide up into Kraler's Corvette and Viper's Lamborghini. They drive through most of the city before reaching their destination – a big house similar to the manors one sees in horror films. The darkness adds to the lugubrious aspect of it and the place seems abandoned, derelict. Gazing up, Angel swallows. *What a gloomy place!*

"Is it here?" she asks Kral upon getting out of the car.

"Yes."

Camilla moves closer to Angel while all the occupiers of the Lamborghini join them.

"Dark and Friz, stand guard," Kral decides.

The two vampires take out their guns and go hunch in the shadows. They've already come here before but they'd be crazy not to cover their asses. Kraler often tells two of his men to stay near the entrance of the house. Just in case the geneticist might want to double-cross him. Then again, it wouldn't really matter. He would be instantly killed by the blade of the Snake leader's favorite dagger.

"Females, get in the car. Don't move or make any noise."

Angel would have preferred to stay near Kral, but she agreed to obey his orders without protesting. Therefore, she pulls Camilla by the arm and they both hide inside the Corvette.

"Let's go!" Kral says to Viper and Slash.

The three vampires climb up the stairs of the horror house and disappear behind its huge black door.

Hidden behing the front seats of the Corvette, Angel and Camilla have to squeeze – there isn't much room in the back area of this kind of sports car. They can see the vampires lurking in the shadows, which is more or less reassuring. They have no idea what they are doing here and would have probably preferred to stay at the manor. If the Snakes' plan goes wrong, they could get in serious trouble or in the worst case, die. The vampires need to collect the syringes but what's inside of them? And what's with their plan to go outside as soon as the sun comes up? Everybody knows the daylight is lethal for them.

"The attack they want to launch scares me," Angel admits.

Camilla doesn't reply anything. She heard about their plan, she doesn't understand it either and she is just as worried as her sister. Worried about Slash. And also about Angel, who loves Kraler. Seems like he's completely lost his mind on that one. However, she tries to put up a front, knowing that her friend needs to stay calm.

"Kral is also scared, if you want to know what I think," Angel adds.

"Why?"

"He wants us to get married just before. That leads me to believe that he might get killed."

"He just wants to marry you because he knows he'll be super busy in the next few days."

"I don't know."

"Stop worrying, Angel. I think it doesn't do you or Kraler any good, right now."

"I know. Now isn't the time to start panicking."

She shuts her eyes and tries to breathe normally, squeezing her sister's hand.

The geneticist welcomes the three vampires in his lab, which is in the basement of the big house. Not wasting any time, he shows them the two suitcases containing the four hundred syringes they ordered. Kraler smiles. That should definitely help them push the soldiers away. It is even more precious to him than a suitcase full of money or diamonds. "Viper, give the doc his money."

The vampire gives him a bag full of bills. The geneticist is over the moon. Corrupted, but over the moon. And he isn't the only one. The three vampires can already smell victory... and what a sweet smell!

"I want some more," Kraler declares. "As many as you can, as soon as possible."

"I shall start right after you leave, my Lord."

Kraler glances at Viper. Lately, he's been brown-nosing him by calling him that. The fact that the geneticist is starting to do this as well leads him to believe that, despite being a human, he might prefer their race. "We have things to do," Kral says. "It is a pleasure to do business with you, doc."

Still on guard, the vampires exit the lab with their two suitcases.

The group leave the manor without a problem. They are now driving towards the temple – out of the city and into the mountains.

"What was it that you had to collect?" Angel asks Kraler.

"Syringes."

"Empty ones?"

"Of course not."

"May I ask what's inside of them?"

"Yes, you may. Inside of them is a product that was made by a geneticist I hired a few months ago."

"What does it do?"

He smiles. *She's so curious!*

"That is none of your business – warrior stuff."

"I won't tolerate to be sidelined."

Camilla thinks Angel is very brave, talking to a vampire as threatening as Kraler in that way. Even though she sleeps with him, that doesn't mean he can't kill her with a snap of the fingers. She respects and admires Kraler's composure. He could send her packing instead of explaining things to her. As times goes by, he goes back up in her estimation. Maybe he's not that bad. With Angel, at least. He's still a blood-thirsty, power-hungry vampire when it comes to the rest.

"I thought you were smarter... but hey, you're just a brainless human after all," he laughs.

"Very funny! I'm not inferior to you."

"Prove it."

He smiles – he isn't angry – just teasing her. However, Angel doesn't like the joke very much. He considers humans as inferior to his race! She will prove him wrong. If the vampires attacked during the day, they would certainly die. But since that is what Kral seems to have planned, there must be something in the suitcase that will help them survive the sun.

"It's a product that will protect you from the sun."

"Actually, the doc is an expert on genetic manipulation. He was able to isolate the gene responsible for the desintegration of vampires in the sun. Those little vials contain an agent inhibiting the gene during twelve hours."

"I was close."

"True."

"Are you sure they're efficient?"

"I paid a lot of money for these."

"Tell me you're going to test these on your warriors before going out in the sun."

"I'm not crazy," he smiles.

She feels reassured.

The cars park in front of the temple and everybody gets out. The girls follow the vampires, who follow Kraler. The double-gate swings open as they stand before it. Yassin was expecting them. He is not only about to welcome the Snake leader and the Council in his temple, but he is also going to marry the Lord to his fiancée. He could not be more honored.

"My Lord," he greets Kraler.

He greets the other vampires with similar respect and then lays eyes on the two females. Humans? He was expecting to meet vampire females, but whatever. He doesn't feel any less flattered.

"Angel and I would like to get married as soon as the meeting is over."

"That would be a great honor, my Lord."

"Have all the warriors been tattooed?"

"The tattoo artists are currently inking the last ones of them, right now."

Kraler nods. The vampires head for the auditorium as Yassin gathers the Snake warriors. Angel and Camilla stay on the side but watch carefully as the vampire leader delivers his speech.

"I have brought something that will protect us from the sun during twelve hours," Kraler explains as Viper and Slash bring the suitcases with the precious elixir inside. He goes on, telling them about the soldiers' evil plan to destroy them and their own plan to counter them. Of course, they all want to save their neighborhood but also defend their territory in the name of the one they consider as their Lord. Not wanting to waste any more time, Kraler tells them about the action plan. "I want everyone on the roofs of the buildings. I want vampires hiding in the dark at every street corner before dawn. As soon as the sun comes up, give yourselves an injection and when you see the first soldiers show up: attack! Kill them all!"

Yassin takes hold of the four hundred syringes to distribute before the warriors will have to leave in a few hours. Kraler climbs down from the platform, followed by the members of the Council.

"This way, my Lord," Yassin says.

The five vampires and the two human girls trail after him.

CHAPTER 32

Wearing a long black dress, Angel joins Kraler in a big, unknown room. He is also wearing black, just like all the other vampires and Camilla. Kral grabs her hand and they walk together toward Yassin and two other vampires dressed in white. They kneel down as Yassin starts speaking in a foreign language that Angel doesn't understand. Kraler closes his eyes, squeezing her hand in his and relishing every word the vampire is saying. He then lets go of his bride-to-be's hand. The union ritual goes on.

Yassin switches to the language that Angel speaks. "According to vampiric customs, I shall first talk to the female. Angeline Amberita, do you promise faithfulness, honor and devotion to Kraler Davers-Snake?"

"I promise."

Kraler opens his eyes and gazes at Angel as he reaches for her hand again.

"Kraler Davers-Snake, do you wish to honor Angeline Amberita by accepting her as your wife?"

Angel notes that the promise isn't the same at all. She promises to be faithful and devoted to him, and all he does is "accept to honor her". Apparently, females are inferior to their husbands in the vampire society.

"I accept to do her that great honor."

"By this gesture and by these words, they accept to become a couple," Yassin declares.

He beckons to two men dressed in black and they step forward. Completely clueless and unknowing of this kind of "wedding", Angel doesn't know what to expect.

"You are going to receive the ultimate symbol of your union sealed forever."

Kral releases the young woman's hand as one of the two men kneels down before him and the other one before her. She casts him a puzzled glance, wondering what she is supposed to do. She sees him hold out his left hand, so she does the same. The man takes her hand. A shiver runs down her spine as she spots the tattoo needle he is holding. Cutting through her skin, he draws a wedding band around her left ring finger – an indelible mark which will let the other vampires know that she is taken. Unfortunately, the soldiers and humans in general will know too, since they are not unaware of this kind of union.

Once the band has been etched in their skin, Yassin declares them husband and wife according to the customs of their vampiric rituals. Kraler concludes the ceremony by kissing shyly his new bride. They both stand up, their knees a bit numb.

"Must she receive your mark right now?" Yassin enquires.

His mark? Now what is that?

If it means "intercourse", then she is more than happy about it.

"Yes," Kral affirms.

"Where would you like the snake to be etched?"

The snake? That doesn't sound like intercourse!

"The wives always have it in the same place. In the hollow of their backs."

Yassin asks his men to bring a foam table.

"I know you're going to find this painful but I'll stay with you," Kral whispers to Angel.

She slowly realizes that she is about to get a tattoo in the hollow of her back. So that was what Yassin was talking about. His mark? A snake, of course. Everyone will be able to see that she belongs to him, after that. She lies down on her stomach without a word. Kraler sits down on a chair next to her while everybody else gets out of the room. He puts his hands on the table, in front of his wife's face, and locks fingers with her.

"If it hurts, you can just bite me," he suggests, showing one of his wrists.

"Be careful," she smiles.

She feels the needles cut through her skin and grits her teeth as the snake uncoils in her back. The clan's symbol. The leader and the members of the Council have it in their backs, the warriors have it on the bicep of their left arm and the wives in the hollow of the back. Kraler senses her pain but she bites the bullet. He is proud of her – she is crushing his fingers but her mouth is closed.

"I'll take your mind off the pain, you'll see," he murmurs in her ear.

"And when I'm done with you, you won't be able to move an inch."

"I have a vague memory of a similar event that happened earlier today."

"Vague?" she smirks. "Wait till we're in your room and I'll refresh your memory."

He kisses her hands despite the presence of the tattoo artist – they will erase his memories before sending him back home anyway.

180

As soon as they walk through the manor's door, Kraler tells his friends that he and Angel are going to bed.

"Don't wear yourself out, boss! We need you to be in great shape when the sun comes up!" Viper snickers.

"Mind your own business, dude! It's my wedding night, I'm going to do every dirty thing you could possibly think of!"

The couple disappears upstairs and Camilla casts a glance at Slash. Watching her, Viper decides to give the stubborn human temptress another lesson. He walks up to Slash and whispers something in his ear. The sound of his voice is too low for Camilla to hear but Slash perceives it perfectly thanks to his over-developped ears.

"Do you care for your family jewels?"

"Uhm... yes. What do you want?"

"Help you preserve them."

Dark and Friz wish them a good night before going upstairs to their rooms, hoping they will get some sleep for at least an hour or two. Vampires don't need to sleep very much – two hours are enough for them to wake up energized and at the top of their capacities.

"Do what you have to do," Slash declares.

Viper smirks before sensually licking the vampire's ear. "Show me some love," he whispers.

Slash wraps his arms around his friend and without warning, Viper kisses him right in front of Camilla, causing her to storm out of the room.

"Do you want me in your bed?"

"It's alright, you made her leave."

"But she's a tough one!"

"I know."

"So what do you reckon, dude? Why should the new couple be the only ones to get laid?"

Slash smiles before telling his friend to follow him.

Kraler makes sure the door is locked before jumping onto the bed like a kid. He is completely naked and lies down, giving himself to his new official partner.

"Those vows were so not equitable," she points out.

"They're just old texts. In those times, it wasn't about the feelings. The female was to shut up and let her man make all the decisions."

She undresses and joins him, lying on top of him. He switches their positions easily, topping her instead.

"I promise you unfailing faithfulness, eternal love and total devotion. I love you, Angeline Amberita."

She smiles, deeply moved by his words. "I love you so much, Kral."

He presses his lips against her, kissing her fervently. He then kisses her throat, her breasts, her stomach and finally, her crotch. He eats her out for a while, making her moan loudly, and then deprives her of his tongue, replacing it with his erected penis. She arches her back to let him in deeply. He starts thrusting in and our of her, varying rhythm and intensity, before pulling out and licking her out again playfully. He explores her intimately for a while, which helps him calm down a bit and not get too excited too fast – what he wants is to make the pleasure last and transform their intimate embrace into a sensual rhapsody.

After having licked the soft, warm and wet flesh inside of her, he penetrates her with his sex again, their bodies fitting together. She quickly climaxes as he pulls out and rolls on the side, drawing her with him. She impales herself on his hard cock and decides on the rhythm, going slowly at first and gradually speeding up, driving him insane. She wants him all for herself and likes to dominate him at times. She ends the penetration, kisses his throat, his torso and stomach, and runs her tongue across his sex before wrapping her mouth around it. He lets her be in charge for a short while, because he knows that he will completely lose control if he lets her take things in hand for too long. He lies her on the bed, penetrating again. He is about to explode – he knows that he will climax soon but he wants to delay the moment and satisfy another need beforehand.

"I want to... drink your blood."

"I told you I want to have you according to your customs."

He slows down, holding back, and kisses her throat before brushing his sharp fangs against her soft skin. He is dying to bite her and drain her blood. With great effort, he lifs up his head and locks eyes with Angel. "Where would you like to drink from me?"

"We could both drink from each other's throat."

A claw appears on his fingers – she had no idea he had that power. He cuts himself below the chin before moving closer to her lips, letting her draw the warm blood from his throat. He pounds her harder suddenly as she hugs him tightly, digging her nails into his back. He lets out a moan, feeling his animal instincts take over. He likes it. He licks her throat before sinking his fangs into her soft skin and sucking her blood vigorously but with infinite tenderness. They drink from each other's throat as he comes inside of her.

She is delicious. Her blood is so exquisite he carries on drinking for a bit longer. He manages to stop himself when he knows it is time. He gives a few licks to the two little holes so they can heal properly. Angel stops drinking as he sucks her finger and then places it over the wound he inflicted on himself.

"You are mine forever, Angel. I shall never do these things with any other female but you."

"Do you want me to be your only source of blood?"

"It would be an honor for me to feed only from my wife."

"I want your blood inside my veins, and you shall have mine running in yours."

He smiles at her, taking this as a definite "yes". He couldn't dream of a more passionate relationship with the woman he is madly in love with. His sex is still inside of her, wanting her again and again. Kraler isn't finished with her, and she sure isn't finished with him either.

Cover illustration by Virginie Wernert
Front cover by Les éditions Sharon Kena
Image credits: dreamstime.com

Printed and bound by lulu.com
June 2014

Publisher n° 917089-36540
Registration of copyright: June 2014

www.ingramcontent.com/pod-product-compliance
Lightning Source LLC
Chambersburg PA
CBHW071912220626
47052CB00002B/315